By Gian De Torre and Mike Brennan
Technical Advisor Richard Stiennon

Cyber Styletto LLC • Sparta, Michigan

YVONNE TRAN

ISBN-13: 978-0-9838261-1-8

Character artwork by Shannon Mash
Cover design by Bookcovers.com

Typefaces: Baskerville and Arial Narrow

Prologue

1 a.m., Tuesday, Dec. 18, 2012, Los Gatos, California

From a few hundred feet away the intersection looked completely clear. In fact, there was no other traffic visible in any direction, which was no surprise for the late hour.

It was tough for the driver to steer, what with seven partiers crammed into a sedan that seated five, but everyone had to get back to the dorms, and this was the only ride available. When they piled in he couldn't say no. He wished they'd quiet down a little, though, and let him focus on the road.

Maybe he'd had one too many himself, but he was doing okay— not speeding, and hadn't crossed any yellow lines so far. Besides, the rest of them had been drinking more heavily.

As they neared the intersection the driver realized the traffic signal was out. There were three—one on the right, one on the opposite corner, and one overhead—and they were all out. That was strange. Signals usually flashed when they weren't working, right? He eased off the accelerator, but they were already into the intersection.

A quarter way through he saw it—they all saw it—a tanker truck bearing down on them.

There wasn't even time for them to close their eyes.

The residents of the apartment building who came out when the cops and paramedics arrived said it sounded more like an explosion than an accident, like a bomb had been dropped from a fighter jet. It took three companies to control the blaze, which burned until almost noon the next day. All seven in the car were incinerated, most beyond recognition. The driver of the rig was killed too.

All the signals in a ten-square-mile area of the city had gone out at the same time. The automatic backups, rigged to keep the red and yellow lights flashing, didn't work. According to the staff at CalTrans, which controlled the new synchronized system, their monitors showed everything was working properly at the time of the accident.

Network Systems had provided the server that ran the synchronization. All functions were automated. Human error had been removed. If a single signal went down, a rare occurrence to begin with, the others in the intersection were programmed to stay on. Traffic management was on its own grid, so if the power in an area went out, signals still did their job. At worst, if an entire intersection somehow went offline, the computers were set to make the lights flash, to warn drivers of the potential danger. In short, the accident should not have happened. It could not have happened.

YVONNE'S KEY WEST BUNGALOW

Chapter 1

4 a.m., Tuesday, Dec. 18, 2012, Yvonne Tran's bedroom

Theirs was a relationship based on advantage—who held it and when, and how strongly. When Stokes called her, she knew it was hers, and she was not about to let him forget it.

She let the refrain from "Satisfaction" play once more on her smart phone before answering.

"You want something, darling?"

He paused for a moment. The trace of her Russian accent always did that to him, no matter how critical the situation. "There's a problem," he said.

"You mean aside from you waking me up at four in the morning?"

"Yes."

"Let me guess. Your wife threw you out again…"

He exhaled slowly into the receiver and she sensed his frustration. Good. Keep the pressure on.

"No, Yvonne. There was an accident in Silicon Valley. Eight people were killed."

"My God. What happened?"

"Something infiltrated an automated traffic system. No one out there has a clue as to who or how."

It was rare that anyone had a clue. That was the common denominator among governments and corporations. She'd dealt with enough of them—for and against—and had yet to encounter an organization that had the slightest idea as to how the world really worked.

"Is this a bad time, Yvonne? I mean, did you just get in? I know how you like to party."

How quickly he could shift gears. But if she recapped the evening's activities, she'd be open. She'd cede control to him. He wanted those details, maybe more than he wanted to discuss this latest crisis. Maybe there was no crisis, and he was merely using a terrible power outage as an excuse for calling, for trying to put her on the defensive, gain an opening so he might make one more pitch to keep their affair going.

"Those files are sealed, Rohan," she said.

"Sorry. Just trying to be nice."

"Can we get to the point?"

She had trusted him, for a little while at least, but how much trust could be generated between a black hat wanted on two continents and a top-level cyber security wonk. Both his government job and her freelance hacking career demanded constant lies and cover-ups, interactions that lasted only hours, rarely days, never longer. She knew an affair couldn't last, and tried to tell him that, to make him see why they shouldn't be together. And then he let it slip that he was married, and that ended it, despite his pleading. Yet he never stopped trying. Even now, with all those people dead and a critical system compromised, he was trying to lead her there.

"That's all I can tell you on this line," he said. "We're not secure. Lieutenant Cummings from my office is on his way to your place. He'll install a Scan-U unit so we can have a conference call."

"Another toy? What does this one do?"

"Holographic communications. 3-D conferencing. This technology allows us to look around corners in someone's room while we're speaking to them."

She knew he was kidding—maybe. "So when you're talking to me you can see what I'm wearing below the monitor."

"Or not wearing."

He was relentless. But she wouldn't let him get off the subject. "CyberCom should be ashamed at how they use the taxpayers' money. Send your Cummings, Rohan. I'll contact you when he's done."

"One more thing," he said. "Cummings will also deliver a small upgrade for your cochlear implant. Just some software you can install in the chip to give you more range."

An hour later she signaled Stokes that her Scan-U unit was activated. He responded, and his holographic image resolved in the space between her and the monitor. For a moment it was a surprise, as if he'd stepped through the screen into her bedroom. The 3-D projection of his head came complete with his mop of brown hair and wire rim glasses. It turned left to right, appearing to scan the room, and her, and Cummings, who was in there too, sipping from a cup of coffee she had offered. She assumed her image was doing something similar on the other end of the communication, and that Stokes was probably running his hand along the electrons that formed the likeness of her hip.

This would not do. She didn't see the value of such a system, except to give Stokes access to her private life. Instead of addressing him straight on, she kept her head down, staring at the keyboard while she worked at hacking the system's code. "So, what else can you tell me, Rohan? You didn't call just to give me that terrible news."

Stokes wasn't ready for business yet. "Is that Cummings?" he asked.

"Yes. He looked a little sleepy."

"So you invited him into your bedroom?"

The officer was leaning against a dresser, downing the last dregs from his cup.

Stokes's voice raised an octave. "And you're still wearing a robe?"

"He is cute. And besides, where else would I set up this new toy? This is where I spend most of my time." While she spoke, she barely lifted her eyes from the Scan-U's controls, but she could sense the scowl creeping over his face. She was enjoying playing with him.

"Yvonne, you should have put the unit in your office. You can't bring my officers into your bedroom."

"Why not? He's not married."

Stokes cleared his throat. His voice came back down to its usual tenor. "Lieutenant, you're only supposed to be there until we're sure the Scan-U is working. As you can see, it is. Now get the hell back to your office!"

There was a fading, "Sir, yes sir!" as Cummings retreated.

When he was gone, Stokes blew another puff of air. "All right, Yvonne," he said. "Time to be serious. Very serious."

"Yes, the signals are still down in Silicon Valley, the police are going crazy trying to control traffic, and Network Systems suspects someone has hacked their command servers."

"How the hell do you know all that?"

"I'm very popular with the boys out there, too. You know how it is—a little smile, a little shake, and some of them will tell you anything." She waited for him to calm down. "Actually, I have some friends at NetSys. They texted me 15 minutes ago." She grabbed her wireless from the table and waved it slowly back and forth. Stokes shook the specter of his head again.

"NetSys says it wasn't just that the signals went out in most of the area," he said. "They weren't able to reroute to get back online. It was almost as if someone else had gained full control. Like they were testing to see how much control they could get."

"A network attack."

"That's what we're looking at."

"Give me some IPs and I'll start looking."

"Hang on. I'm bringing in my boss, Vice Admiral Lucas from CyberCom, and a Mr. Sanchez."

"Right now?" she replied.

"Yes."

"A girl can't sleep in anymore. All right."

As Stokes moved to conference in the other parties, Yvonne finished accessing Scan-U's program. She copied a few lines of code from a routine on her personal computer, and configured it to replace the command that instructed the unit to take video of her and project it to the others in the conference. She ordered it to instead access a file she had stored on the web.

"What the f...?" Stokes said.

"Language, darling. We have guests." An artist friend of hers had created an animation a few weeks before at her request—a fantasy superhero—raven haired, with a face like a princess, and an athlete's body wrapped in a leather jumpsuit, wearing four-inch heels. It was not that different from her real appearance, but having this alter ego to present to strangers made her more comfortable. She could control the image from her own keyboard, and make the 3-D graphic respond to her commands. She commanded the cartoon body to swivel seductively, and knew it would produce the same show for everyone else in the conference. "I needed to do something about my appearance," she said. "I just look a mess at this hour." She had to laugh at her own joke. "Besides, you don't want to divulge my identity just yet, right?"

"But how did you do that? The Scan-U is the most advanced piece of communications technology at CyberCom. It's completely new."

"Nothing a good hacker can't figure out. That's why you hire me, remember?"

She sometimes thought the real reason was because he was still in love with her, but it was far more involved. Beyond his little boy infatuation was a mind as duplicitous as hers—almost. She wasn't just a hacker, he'd told her, she was the best he'd ever confronted. He was CIA at the time. He and his team pursued, and she eluded. She flirted with him as she ridiculed their efforts, and he had the gall to flirt back. The men she duped usually became angry that a woman could outsmart them, but Stokes seemed to enjoy the competition. And then they caught her, and as she was brought into custody she could not help thinking she had let herself be caught, if only to meet him, to see in person a man who played the game at her level. Now she owed him for keeping her out of prison. She could have been hacking into another online scam, ripping off the ripoff artists and making a million or so in the process, but she was stuck working for Stokes, chasing what was probably a short circuit or a tripped breaker somewhere. She chastised herself again for her mistakes—playing with him, leaving herself open, getting involved. They were mistakes she promised never to make again.

Two new holographic images appeared simultaneously, on either side of Stokes. Ed Lucas was on the left. Almost a pity he was in the military. He had the ruddy good looks that would have made him a decent model—or a porn star. On the right was a woman in a suit, with her hair pulled back into a bun so tight it raised the corners of her eyebrows into a Mr. Spock-like air of astonishment. Maybe Stokes had made a mistake referring to her in the masculine, but Yvonne couldn't let it go—anyone this stiff deserved derision.

"My dear Edward," Yvonne said. "So nice to see you again. And this must be Mr. Sanchez."

The woman huffed. "What? That's Ms. Sanchez."

"Really?"

"My fault. Totally my fault," Stokes cut in. "Someone on my staff must have made a typo in the message he sent, and I passed it on."

"An honest blunder, I'm sure," Yvonne said. "The mistake is certainly understandable."

"Where's her image?" Sanchez said. "All I'm getting is an avatar. It looks like some kind of Spider-woman."

"Ooh, that's a new one," Yvonne said. "I like it. I think maybe I will use it."

"I need to see her face!"

"Sorry, darling, that image is classified."

"Mr. Stokes, who is this person?"

Yvonne smiled. She had Sanchez off balance and would keep her that way. It made the stuffed shirts and blouses so much easier to deal with.

Stokes cut in. "Ms. Sanchez, I can't divulge this person's name. She's a cyber security expert with top-secret clearance and a record of cracking some of our most difficult cases. Her code name is Cyber Styletto."

The avatar curtsied.

Sanchez let out a "Humph."

"Besides, as Rohan knows, I look a fright when I get out of bed," Yvonne said.

"Do you have to make those jokes?"

"Oh yes, Rohan. It makes me... how do you say... more human."

"Please, the situation is critical."

"All right," Yvonne said. "I will focus. So who is the lovely lady?"

"Rita Sanchez, chief information security officer at Network Systems, the company that sold the servers to CalTrans."

"Time to check the warranty. Maybe CalTrans can get a refund."

"I swear, Miss...Miss. Oh, never mind," Stokes said.

"Ms. Sanchez," Stokes said, "can you fill us in on what you've been able to determine?"

Sanchez had nothing. Instead she rattled on about product performance and redundancies, and how the servers were designed to be virtually impossible to compromise. She played with the top button of her blouse, which seemed to Yvonne to be tight enough to choke her.

While she listened to the woman fumble for answers, Yvonne reached for the computer keyboard on her desk and tapped in a few more commands. Network System's files were password protected, with redundancies, but her password generator cracked through before Sanchez finished speaking. She conducted a few file searches, and a schematic of the traffic control grid in the area displayed. She traced the signal outages with her fingers, looking for patterns. Sanchez went on, and she interrupted. "This is definitely an attack, but it's also a probe."

"What do you mean?" Sanchez asked.

"They're looking for weaknesses more than trying to cause damage at this point. Whoever did it may have been surprised they were able to control the system so easily. That's why the attack came in the middle of the night. If they wanted to hurt people they would have done it during rush hour."

"They found a way to hurt people anyway," Stokes said.

"The attackers probably consider that collateral damage."

"Is this the work of a foreign power?" Lucas asked.

"Maybe. Maybe not."

"This is like the Bay Area power outage in 2001," Lucas said. "We knew that one was a state-sponsored probe. They were testing our security protocols."

"It's a very sophisticated attack," Yvonne said. She typed out more commands. A portion of the Network Systems server motherboard came into focus on the screen, and she relayed it into the Scan-U system so the others could see. "Ms. Sanchez, I need you to send me the complete schematic of this."

"My God. How did you get that?" Sanchez said.

"Your networks are not as secure as you might think. How soon can I have it?"

Stokes cut in. "I think you'll agree our agent needs to take over this investigation as soon as possible."

"You know my price, Rohan."

"I'll have a quarter million dollars deposited in your account as soon as the bank opens this morning. You get the other quarter million when the job is completed…to our satisfaction."

"And I want an extra quarter million from Network Systems. For, um, consulting."

Sanchez hand went from her button to her throat. "What? That's extortion," she said.

"And you'll pay it," Stokes said. "If you want to keep supplying servers to CalTrans and other government agencies."

Sanchez turned away and seemed to be muttering something to an associate. Admiral Lucas had to bring a hand up to hide his laughter. "I see our agent hasn't changed a bit since she started working for us. Still as mercenary as ever," he said.

ROHAN STOKES

Chapter Two

Noon Wednesday, Dec. 19, 2012, Key West, Florida

Yvonne banked her corporate jet east, towards the Key West runway. A line of dark clouds, heavy with moisture, loomed to the southeast. Radar had it moving towards the islands, due in an hour or so. It would be a race to pick up the server NetSys had shipped and get back to her bungalow before the rains made it virtually impossible to drive—having a place in the Keys had its disadvantages sometimes.

"Sorry, Red Bird." It was Ralph in the tower. "I've got two ahead of you. GA to the south so I can get these folks in."

"Listen, darling," Yvonne said. "This one's urgent. Can you give me priority?"

"What's up? In a hurry to get to Finnegan's? I can't be there 'til later, you know."

"I'll see you then, but right now I've got a bit of a crisis."

"Like what?"

"Can't tell you. Sorry."

"Then I'm sorry too. Take it out and loop back in twenty."

Yvonne pushed the twin throttles forward and the jet surged towards the airport, passing within a quarter mile of a fifty-seater, filled most likely with tourists, people who had a lot more time to waste than she did. The pilot of the other jet banked hard to pull off his glideslope. Yvonne heard him bellow into the radio, "Tower, I've got an unauthorized flight in close proximity. What the hell are you doing down there?"

"Yvonne!" Ralph screamed. "I told you to go around."

She ignored him and swooped the jet in hard, as though she were landing on an aircraft carrier. As soon as it touched down she hit the brakes and the reversers until the jet shuddered to a stop. Then she turned the craft and taxied it right up to the terminal. Two security cars, lights flashing, followed her in and pulled up next to the plane. A small crowd gathered at the security checkpoint inside to watch the officers escort her from the tarmac to inside.

Yvonne grinned as they led her past the onlookers. A middle-aged man in shorts, a cabana shirt and a Detroit Tigers baseball cap covering his graying hair pushed his way to the front of the group and waved. "Nice show, Yvonne," he said.

"Sock! My old friend. Thanks for meeting me here. Can you do me a small favor, darling?"

"It'll cost you."

She stopped to chat. Instead of pushing her forward, the security men allowed it, as though they were beginning to understand she was no average scofflaw.

"Doesn't it always?" she said. "I'll buy you a drink at Finnegan's tonight."

"You know I come cheap, baby. What's the favor?"

"I'm in a bit of a hurry. Can you bring my car around?" She tossed him the keys.

Sock took off his hat and scratched his head. "Looks like you might be awhile."

"Five minutes," she said. "Meet you outside. And have the boys take the jet to the hangar. I'll make it two drinks."

One of the officers nudged her towards a private room for questioning. When they cleared the crowd, he asked, "Sock?"

"Dutch Sock Van Dorp," she said. "Second best pilot in the state." She didn't have to tell them who was first.

The door to the little room clicked shut, and the second security man pulled a metal chair out for her. "Okay, miss…"

"I won't need it," she said. "And neither will you." She sat on a corner of the table and crossed her legs, making sure the curve of her hip in the tight jeans was in the guard's vision. She pulled a leather cardholder from her jacket pocket and pulled out the first card.

"CIA?" the first officer said. "I wish you people would just let us know you were coming. It would save a lot of hassle."

"Yes, but if we tell you what we're up to, we wouldn't be a secret organization anymore." She slipped the card back into its place, hiding similar identifications for the FBI, National Security Agency, Homeland Security, MI6, NATO, and a few others that had come in handy over the years.

The cop looked her over. "So how does one get involved in the secrets business?" he asked.

He was fairly cute. Muscular, at least. "Stop by Finnegan's Wake tonight after nine and maybe I'll explain it."

"The Irish place?"

She winked at him. Cliché, she knew, but it rarely failed.

Minutes later, Yvonne walked out of the terminal, still holding the stares of the security team and most of the crowd that had watched her come in. The Porsche was parked at the end of the taxi queue and Sock stood by the passenger door, twirling the keys around his finger. A woman in a man's shirt and jeans waved. "Taxi, Yvonne?"

"Teivel! Would love to, but I stashed my car here when I left. Have to make a quick getaway."

"Finnegan's, then? Tonight?"

"Of course."

She walked quickly down the line of cars to Sock. "Looks like it'll be a full house tonight, darling."

"Nice to see you can still mix pleasure with business," he said, tipping his cap like a chauffeur.

Yvonne started the Porsche and creeped it past the pedestrian crosswalk. As soon as the tailpipe cleared the yellow line she floored it, and was in fifth gear before the airport exit. The post office on Whitehead should have the server by now, if the idiots at Network Systems hadn't tried to save a few dollars by sending it bulk rate. Despite the rush to beat the storm, Yvonne had an urge to take the long way to the PO. The daredevil flight hadn't been enough of a thrill, and she knew if she swung over to the Causeway she could hit ninety if there wasn't too much traffic and the police were taking their usual afternoon siesta. But if she went that way, she'd want to stop at her bungalow first, and that would mean she might not beat the weather. The black horizon made the decision for her. It was going to be a bad one.

At the Post Office her friend Thomas had the shipment waiting. "I've already reserved a table at the Wake for tonight," he said as she walked in.

"Wonderful! But you'd better make it two tables. Looks like we're going to have quite a group tonight."

He abandoned his counter and the three other customers waiting to be served to help her load the box into the passenger seat of the car.

"Network Systems," he said, reading the label. "More computer equipment?"

"Special order." She patted the box. "With this one I'll be able to see inside your house when I email you."

Thomas laughed and went back inside. Yvonne recalled the Scan-U phone conference earlier at her Long Island condo—it might not be too long before her statement became true.

Yvonne drove the few blocks back to her street, then through the alley to her garage. The dark entry sometimes made her think of her life as a superhero's; she was Batgirl, only with less risk and more friends. She'd only been on the ground less than an hour and already had a crew lined up for the evening's fun, including that hunky security cop. Yet that reminded her of another similarity she had to a brooding crime fighter—her life was never as happy as it should have been. Despite the demands for her talents at work and her presence at parties, memories of the Russian half of her family helped keep happiness in check.

But no time to dwell on that. She brought the box upstairs and unpacked the server, then hooked it to her system, and watched and listened as it powered up. Typical Network Systems software—clunky, but it got the job done. Nothing wrong at first glance.

A ripple of thunder echoed outside. The storm was almost over the Keys. She was sorry to have scared those tourists back in the air over the runway, but now she was glad she'd made the move. It allowed her to be back here, dry and working. Those poor saps were probably running for their motel rooms right about now. People who sat back and let others have control of a situation were always taken advantage of. She hadn't let that happen in a long time, not since Stokes and his team took her in. She needed a drink.

But it was only five. She'd be out later with the crowd at Finnegan's. Oh well, she'd just get an early start.

When she went down to the bar to mix a stinger, the storm hit with full force. It wasn't a hurricane, but it was in the ballpark. She wouldn't be surprised if the power went...

Sure enough, the lights in her bungalow flickered for a few seconds, went out and then came back on as the auxiliary generator in her garage sensed the outage and fired itself up. She had battery backup, so the computer system was secure, but she thought she heard the server reboot, and raced upstairs to check.

Everything looked the same, but something was working differently. She could hear it in her cochlear implant. Good old Dr. Malakhov. He had no idea his little sound amplifier would turn out to be so useful. It was supposed to help her childhood hearing problem, but it had done so much more. Yvonne pushed her drink to the edge of the table, closed her eyes and focused. An array of electrical impulses flooded her mind. She visualized an aurora of color and wave patterns, each image corresponding to an activity within the server. Yes, there was an anomaly. The patterns had shifted since the power went out and the system rebooted. It was on the motherboard. Something there that shouldn't be. She found a screwdriver. A closer inspection was in order.

She removed the server's shell amid the noise and lightning flashes of the storm overhead, then closed her eyes again. The electronic signatures she received through the implant would lead to the anomaly. She followed them. The signals were so close to the originals it was difficult to maintain the trail, especially in the waterfall of information her mind perceived. Even the lightning above was working against her, adding its erratic signals to the ones she sought, like AM radio interference.

Simplify, she thought. She snapped herself out of the trance and turned off everything that didn't have to be running—the monitors, the ancillary computer systems, even her appliances—anything that could produce a signal that would hinder the search.

She reached over and turned off her wireless devices, and turned out the lights in her lab. It was like working in a medieval laboratory; with the lightning overhead it was like something out of Frankenstein. But now she could isolate the signal.

There, in the sector that governed the power supply—a tiny chip. At first she thought it might be a redundancy, something added by Network Systems to guard against one of their inevitable failures. But no, this was not part of the original schematic. Someone had added it after assembly—delicately soldered into the circuits—someone who wanted to be able to gain access to the server command sequence without going through the network interface, who wanted to be able to get in and out undetected. Her joke at the PO hadn't been far from another truth—whoever had implanted this chip would be able to access the very heart of the traffic system's controls.

She opened her eyes. There it was, plain as day, in the middle of the motherboard. She wanted to touch it, to feel its energy. Perhaps by doing so it would impart its secrets and point back to its origins. But that would be stupid. She would have to figure this out the way she always did, with tireless effort, chasing electrons around the globe, and with the intuition born of a lifetime devoted to computer science. She still loved the challenge of matching wits with unseen adversaries, of deducing motives and methods, and figuring their next moves before they did, even if she now had to do it for the government instead of herself. The idea of this as a superhero's life made her laugh—she was Batgirl confined to an Aeron chair. The risks she took on the job were virtual. Yes, she was on the wanted lists of some foreign jurisdictions, but as long as she never visited them, her career wasn't any more dangerous than any corporate executive's. No wonder she couldn't help racing her car and plane when she had the opportunity.

Stokes would want to know what she'd found. Yvonne typed out a secure message, asking him to initiate another Scan-U in the morning. "But not too early, darling," she wrote. "It may be a long night."

A good afternoon's work. Yvonne reached for her stinger and toasted herself in the dark. The last of the storm passed over, and a ray of light shone through her window. Almost dusk. She could knock off now and join the fun at the bar. Some of them were probably there already, waiting for her. It was just a short walk to Finnegan's, so if she and the cop hit it off, it would be convenient to further activities.

But why limit her options? She decided to call Colin Doherty, that young stud pilot she'd met through Buck Ryan's repo service. She didn't want to be alone tonight, and if he came down from the northern Keys it would double her chances. Let them fight over her.

"Colin, darling. Feel like getting out to have some fun?"

"Just say where and when, Yvonne."

"Finnegan's Wake. It's a party."

There was a pause on the other end. "I'm ninety miles away, you know. The weather's still a bit rough for a motorcycle."

"Afraid of a little rain?"

"And fifty-mile-an-hour gusts."

"I see. You're finally settling down. I was wondering when that would happen."

"Damn it. The Ducati is gassed up. I'll be there in two hours. This better be worth it."

"Have I ever disappointed you?"

FINNEGAN'S WAKE

Chapter Three

8 pm Wednesday, Finnegan's Wake

The sounds of the fun at Finnegan's wafted down the alley to Yvonne like an aroma—enticing, pungent with expectation, pulling her in against her better judgment. Maybe she ought to keep working, pinging the mystery chip and pinpointing the origin of its owners. But responsibility faded as she walked through the packed bar. Life in the Keys had its own conventions, one of which was nobody worked nights unless the job was connected to the entertainment. Some people served the alcohol; others imbibed. There wasn't much going on in between, and she liked it that way. Work hard, play hard. This rhythm of island life brought her back here several times a year.

She stopped at the door to the patio and surveyed. Sock, Ralph and Rachel Teivel had commandeered a table—probably showed up at four to make sure they got the best one—and basked in the coast's evening breezes. Thomas pulled a chair out to join them. The rest of the crowd languished, elbow-deep in pitchers of beer. Yvonne saw them as escapees from colder climates and lives they could never quite justify, transported into this Jimmy Buffett reverie, people who may once have had nothing in common, but now shared a healthy disregard for appearances and conformity.

It could have been a grand ball. She might have worn an evening gown instead of jeans and a tank top. Nearly every time she thought about how else her life might have turned out, she imagined the marble halls of her childhood, watching her parents circulate among members of the Politburo and the rest of the Soviet apparatchiks. She pictured her father in his army uniform, the red trim outlining his broad shoulders. Although he held the rank of colonel, he looked far more regal than any of the generals who might attend. Descendants of the previous century's royalty were rare, and he never allowed anyone to forget that a few of the Romanov family had survived the revolution and the purges that came after. Her mother looked like royalty too, her Vietnamese and French looks making her far more exotic than the pale Russians who surrounded her. Together they always outshone whatever the Communists could stuff into a dress or tux. No wonder so many people in Soviet society hated them. Her parents, of course, returned the sentiment in their own way, flaunting their intellects and lineage over the party hacks.

But that was the problem at home too—the rest of her father's family was more concerned with rank and cronyism than character. They made her mother pay for it at every gathering, and made it worse for her, because in the eyes of the aunts, uncles and cousins she was something not completely Russian and never quite good enough in their opinion. She remembered how frightened she became when her parents left her with relatives; how, if she displeased them, they would lock her in a servant's closet for hours. And if she complained to her parents when they returned, the aunts and uncles would say her imagination bordered on insanity. They would insist Yvonne be sent to a psychiatrist, or even an institution.

She rebelled as much as she could, immersing herself in computer science. As soon as she was of legal age she took her mother's maiden name, Tran.

If her father hadn't been assigned to America she might still be over there, enduring familial slights, maybe cracking code for Russian internet thugs, or worse, for the thugs in government. Much better that she stayed here. Life was at least comfortable working for Stokes and his boys, and as she leaned back and put her feet up on Sock's leathery kneecaps, she relaxed in the knowledge that it was so much more casual too.

As much as she loved chasing down electrons, hacking into valuable sites, or nailing the scum that wrote code to infiltrate databases, she appreciated this part of her life just as much. She'd never thought people like Sock, Rachel and Thomas would be her friends, but they were among the few who let her be herself, who could watch her get drunk and pick up some young stud for the night, and never say a word about it the next day. Each time she thought about the pretentious life she might have led back in Moscow she knew she'd made the right decision. Her only regret was having lost touch with her daughter, Lillian, so many years ago. She'd be eighteen soon.

But she wouldn't think about that now. It would put too much of a damper on the good times she planned for tonight.

As she reached to sip her Stoli, an authoritative voice addressed her from behind, through the din coming from the bar. It sounded familiar.

"Miss, I have some questions I'd like to ask you." She turned to see hunky security guy, dressed now in shorts and a muscle shirt. A bit of a bodybuilder, this one.

She ran her fingers along his triceps, feeling the hard symmetry of what she estimated to be four hours a day in the gym. "Not bad," she said. "I have a few questions for you, too, and they have nothing to do with airports."

He picked up Sock's seat—with Sock in it—and moved it two feet to the side so he could slide another chair in. Then he pivoted in next to her and introduced himself as Kyle. That was another thing she loved about the Keys—meeting people, especially men, especially good-looking men, was so easy. Even at forty she had no problem hooking up whenever she wanted.

Sock was fine with the move. In fact, he applauded the display of strength. The six at the table relaxed over drinks as the sun took its time dipping through the persimmon-colored sunset into the gulf. Yvonne caught up on the latest news from Sock and Thomas, while Kyle performed a sitting pose-down for her and Rachel, flexing each time he brought his beer to his lips. The cheap display lessened his chances in Yvonne's mind; but Rachel seemed interested. They were both all about bodies—Rachel looked like she spent a lot of her time in the gym too. Maybe they were made for each other.

Thomas and Sock went on about mundane island events—who was dating whom, who had fallen behind on their house payments, who would attend Finnegan's New Year's party. Sometimes it was hard for Yvonne to get into their blue-collar obsessions. But she had to pretend those things interested her to keep them from guessing about her life. At least it was fun keeping her government work secret.

An hour or so later the sun had set and everyone settled into a pleasant contemplation of the dark, glowing sky. Yvonne nursed her third Stoli. Kyle was on the other side of the table now, and he and Rachel were nuzzling each other like buff thoroughbreds. It was no great loss, as far as Yvonne was concerned. Muscle men looked good, but they were so into themselves it often meant disappointment in bed. Rachel would find out later. The evening seemed to be winding down. Even the loud conversations at the beginning of the evening had quieted to a low buzz.

Inside, someone had found an instrument and began strumming. Whoever had it was merely raking his fingers across the strings, making a racket instead of music. Still, the sound was strangely infectious, reminiscent of another place and time. She recognized it as something from her childhood, something she and her father had shared. Of course! A balalaika. Who had one down here?

Colin came through the doors to the patio like a wandering minstrel—one, however, who had no idea how to play.

"Give me that!" Yvonne said. He did, and she cradled the instrument like it was a baby. "Where did you get it?"

Colin smiled. "The last time we met you told me how you used to play duets with your father back in Moscow. I thought I would surprise you."

"You darling! How nice."

"If you only knew how difficult it was to carry this on my back on the Ducati at ninety miles an hour," he said. "Why don't you play something for us?"

It had been years since she'd even held one, yet the songs she and her father played came back to her as though they had practiced yesterday. Yvonne fingered a few chords. The feel of the strings against her fingers brought it all back to her—afternoons with the winter sun streaming through the window of the Moscow apartment, she and her father on the couch, leaning against each other and taking different parts of the harmony, forgetting, for a while, the next skirmish with the extended family.

Yvonne played "Katyusha." She knew no one in the bar would know what it meant, but for a moment she was back in the living room with her father, playing a song about a lovesick girl watching her man go off to war.

A crowd of people from the bar and patio formed around her. After a while they began to clap along with the rhythm. Yvonne usually didn't care for these kinds of group love-ins, but tonight was different. The world felt good. Colin would be rewarded for his thoughtfulness.

She kept on playing: "Stenka Razin," "Along the Petersburg Road," even "The Volga Boatmen." The audience grew larger, as more people from the front of the bar joined the show. She noticed out of the corner of her eye that Rachel and Kyle were now sitting close with their muscular arms around each other. Funny how her brief infatuation with the muscle man had passed so quickly. And here was Colin, not nearly as buff—a little geeky in fact—and yet right now he seemed to be the sexiest man on the planet.

Yet while she was playing and looking at Colin, it was Stokes's voice she imagined. Yes, they'd had an affair, but now she merely worked for him, and the workday was over too. What would bring him to mind now? She stared at Colin and smiled, but the thought of Stokes wouldn't go away.

"I want to talk to you... now!"

"Rohan?" This wasn't imagination. She heard him speak to her.

"Put down the ukulele and pick up your phone."

"It's not a ukulele, it's a balalaika!" She was shouting now, to no one. The people in the front of the crowd stopped clapping and stared. She stopped strumming.

Colin looked at her as though she was having a breakdown. "Easy, honey," he said. "We know it's a balalaika."

"I ... I'm sorry, everyone," she said. "I was thinking of something and I got carried away."

The faces said they were trying to understand, but still she felt embarrassed. She handed the balalaika back to Colin and headed for the ladies'.

Inside a stall she picked up the smart phone. Stokes was waiting for her. "Rohan, what's going on? How is it I can hear your voice in my head?"

"Must be love, Yvonne. You can't get me out of your mind." She listened as he fought to hold back a laugh.

"My implant!" She touched her jaw. "That was no upgrade. You want to spy on me."

"Think of me as your conscience. A friendly one who only wants to make sure you're okay and working on the case."

"So you can hear everything that's going on?"

"As long as your cell phone is turned on."

"And what if I take Colin home with me tonight? You going to listen in on that too?"

"Your conscience advises you to forget about him."

"Pervert," she said. "I'll have to make some adjustments to your software."

"What kind of adjustments? You can't modify government issue."

"And you can't invade my private life, Rohan. I may work for you, but I'm still allowed to have one, you know." She could hear him struggling to keep his temper. Good. She had the upper hand again.

"Listen," he said. "I don't want to spoil your fun, but the people at Network Systems are on my case to learn the problem with the server. And do I need to mention my superiors at CyberCom would like to see some movement on this too?"

"Rohan, darling, you know no one works nights in the Keys. But I promise I'll get back on it as soon as the sun comes up."

"No later, though. Rita Sanchez has already called me four times today."

"Really. Maybe she has more than computers in mind."

"Not funny, Yvonne."

"All right. Tell Sanchez to hang on. I should have some answers by noon."

Stokes looked relieved. "Good. Then as soon as you figure it out, call me."

She went back to the patio to join the others, but Stokes's reprimand was already doing its intended job, getting her to think about the server problem again. When she had some answers maybe she'd offer to chase the leads down herself. The chip in the server intrigued her. It was the kind of attack she would have conducted herself, back when she freelanced and sold her black hat skills to the highest bidder. Now someone else was enjoying the thrill of the virtual hunt. That irked her, made her a little jealous.

If she could convince Stokes to let her go, she'd need some people she could trust, and that didn't include the stiffs from CyberCom or NSA that Stokes would recommend. Might as well start lining a team up before he could push his own people into the case. Colin would be perfect, in more ways than one. He was nearly as good a pilot as she, and had a decade's worth of experience, even though he was only twenty-nine.

Yvonne took the chair next to Colin and put her head on his shoulder.

"Show's over?" he said.

"Public show," she said. "But there's a private performance a little later."

He rubbed her thigh. "Why wait for the previews when we can leave now?"

"Colin, darling," she said. "I have a proposition for you."

"I thought you'd never ask."

"Actually," she said. "I might have two propositions."

COLIN RUSSELL

Chapter Four

6 a.m., Thursday, Yvonne's Key West Bungalow

Yvonne poured through the maliciously functioning server while Colin slept the night's activities off. It was tough working with a hangover, but nothing she hadn't done before—just a little harder to focus was all. The pounding, claustrophobic sensation left over by her partying made her imagine the server as a cave, with its dark secrets hidden at the bottom of some impossibly obscure passage. Cyber spelunker, she thought, and started to laugh, but laughter was painful this early. A Bloody Mary might not solve the computer mystery, but it would take the edge off her discomfort.

Colin, still naked, met her at the bar. He grabbed her wrist and pulled her towards him, and tried to slip his other hand under her t-shirt, but an elbow to his Adam's apple put a stop to that.

"Hey, honey, what's the matter?"

"Sorry, Col. But duty calls. I've got a renegade chip in that server and Stokes is waiting for an answer."

"You sure?" He turned towards her and flexed his pecs. That wasn't where she was looking, however. "You know you want to," he said.

Yes, she did. But the last thing she needed was another suitor, another hanger-on, calling her when she was working, interrupting when she relaxed with someone else. Her life alone was as good as it could be—apart from her responsibilities to CyberCom she made the decisions about where she went and with whom. She made the kind of money most people could only dream of, had the kind of talent and respect others could never even imagine. She wasn't going to let that be tied down in a relationship, no matter how good looking or important the man was. She wouldn't do it for Colin, and she certainly wouldn't do it for Stokes. If only he were here so she could throw an elbow his way.

"Get dressed, Colin. Bring me a Bloody Mary and then you can make us some breakfast. There's eggs and bacon in the fridge. And don't forget the Tabasco."

He did as he was told. At least dating younger men meant they listened occasionally. But that only reminded her of her age. She didn't want to be anyone's mommy, either. Maybe that's why she'd let Lillian go off to live with her family all those years ago—considering how she'd been treated by the relatives as a child it might not have been the best decision, but then a life spent ignored while mommy glued her gaze to a monitor wouldn't have been good for Lillian either. Yvonne had sent enough money back to Moscow to make sure Lillian received the best education and never wanted for material needs, but she wondered often about her daughter's emotional state. The letters between them were rare, now that Lillian was almost eighteen. God, she was old enough now to date Colin too.

While he rummaged for pans and plates she turned her attention back to the server. How engrossing, this work. In a sense it was liberating too, because it demanded a level of concentration that made life's problems recede into the subconscious. Never mind the dysfunction of her relatives. Never mind the boys and their never-ending games to impress her. This was the chess match. Someone had placed this chip on the motherboard, right under the noses of the Network Systems techs, and hid it and its functions well enough that they never suspected until it turned on and ceded control to a remote commander. And the programming! She hooked the board to her system to read the code embedded within. Layers and layers of commands and parameters, perfectly designed to isolate sub stations and controllers, and avoid detection by feeding dummy readings to the CalTrans sensors. Whoever designed this had to know not only the workings of the server, but those of the entire traffic grid and its stations, in order to know how to shut them down. And the chip made it all easy. It acted as a back door through which the attackers could access at any time, as though they had made a skeleton key that unlocked the traffic control program.

Exquisite.

And as she scanned through thousands of lines of code written in redundant languages—even C and C++—and saw the programmable logic controller rootkit, she knew this was an offspring of Stuxnet, not nearly as involved, but still capable of incredible damage. There was root kit, there the replacement DLLs for the network interfaces. There was the privilege escalation that made it possible to override any attempt by the authorized user to wrest control by changing the root passwords. Since changing the default passwords would disable the server software completely, Network Systems protocols dictated they remain unchanged, giving the worm the opportunity to proliferate exponentially, throughout the system, into any connected device. A single rogue chip might produce access to dozens of critical functions. In any server that had been compromised, infiltration was made ridiculously easy, and could clear the way for additional breeches and takeovers, like falling dominoes—perhaps even some that the chip's designers hadn't even imagined. Who knew what other control systems might be on the verge of failure?

Stuxnet had needed a team of the best engineers to program it— a team at a government level—and not just any government. Even this new variant required a level of understanding and capability at the top of the programming food chain. Could another country be backing this effort to infiltrate critical systems? Stuxnet had helped delay Iran's effort to achieve nuclear power and weapons. Now maybe someone was trying to turn the tables and damage America's infrastructure, and as she and hundreds of experts knew, many of the country's various infrastructure components were already in danger of failing even without the push from Stuxnet. This kind of worm, with some additional engineering, could potentially give control of vital systems to a hostile force. Instead of mere failure, these systems could be made to cause damage—both physical and economic. With crucial systems in someone else's control, the nation could be essentially powerless to protect itself.

She texted Stokes and told him she needed to speak with Rita Sanchez and whoever headed logistics at Network Systems. A few seconds later, he was signaling on the Scan-U, and his 3-D image appeared in front of the monitor.

"You're up early, Rohan."

"Frankly, I've been up for hours waiting for you to tell me something that I can relay to the White House. What have you got?"

"This." She held up the evil chip. "Somebody got a little crazy with the soldering gun."

His electronic head turned to look at it. "Yvonne, did I ever mention you have a gift for understatement?"

"Whoever's behind this plopped this chip right into the middle of the motherboard. And it's so small and so well programmed even I might not have noticed its presence. So of course it had no trouble getting past the Network Systems team."

"I'd better get Rita on the line with us."

"Hmmm," Yvonne said. "Already on a first-name basis? Something going on there?"

"Don't make jokes. You know I don't go for the super bitch type. I like a woman who likes to have fun. Someone with a sense of adventure."

"Too bad you're not very adventurous yourself."

"What? What do you mean?"

It was just a line, but she had touched a nerve.

"Oh come on, Rohan. You sit at a desk all day and push paper and buttons. Once in a while you run off to a meeting. That's not exactly my idea of adventurous."

"Is that why you broke it off with me?"

"Sure, sure, darling. The last time you did field work was when you were with the CIA and arrested me."

"That was a pretty exciting time."

"And I was impressed. I'd been able to keep my activities a secret from the government and the mob. You were the only one who figured me out."

"Yvonne, I'm still trying to figure you out." Stokes paused, then added, "You know, I could get back out there anytime I want."

"Oh yes, Rohan. You just tell the Assistant for Homeland Security and Counterterrorism his top man is taking some time off to chase the bad guys. I'm sure he'll understand."

Colin called to her as he brought two steaming plates from the kitchen. "I have your order, madame. Would you care for another Bloody Mary?"

Stokes's holograph pivoted left, as though by doing so it could see into the kitchen. "Who is that?"

"Oh, just a house guest."

"But he's not wearing a shirt."

Yvonne laughed. "You're lucky he's wearing pants. Colin, say hello to the nice man."

Colin stopped and smiled. "Hello, Rohan." He waved into the screen, and then went back to the bar. She imagined Colin's projection appearing in Stokes's office, shaking a slightly transparent hand in his face.

"He doesn't get to call me Rohan," Stokes said.

"I'll remind him next time he's here."

Stokes puffed his cheeks as though he'd conceded this round of banter. "All right, Ms. Tran, what else can you tell me about this chip?"

"Not much yet. That's why I need the Network Systems people. They may be able to help at last."

"Did you ping the chip's C and C yet?"

"I'll do that while you're getting Ms. Sanchez out of bed... oops! I mean, while you're getting her on the Scan-U."

"Goodbye, Yvonne. I'll signal you in a few minutes."

She put the Scan-U to sleep and brought her breakfast back into the kitchen to join Colin. She found him instead in the living room, hooked up to the huge flat screen Stokes had sent her when they were having their affair. He'd accessed an online community of Armageddon Squadron.

"I'm kicking some serious butt," he said. "Commando style."

"Didn't you get enough of that when you flew drones?"

"There's never enough when you can smell the kill."

If the search for the origin of the chip meant physically tracking down the source, his flying skills, both real and virtual, might be an asset. But he was so young; in many ways still a boy. Maybe she would boot him back to the northern Keys instead.

Yvonne watched as he manipulated a computer generated aircraft while shoveling his scrambled eggs. He had the coordination of an athlete, able to accomplish difficult maneuvers without conscious thought, and she could see how he'd been able to fly the Air Force's drones past enemy defenses and over moon-like terrain to drop ordnance on suspected terrorists. He loved it, practically breathed it. But like her, he found out quickly he could make more money in the private sector. His game really was a game—online flight simulator tournaments, which had made him financially independent. She wasn't unhappy working for the government—and there was even some time to pick up occasional work from cash-rich corporate clients, not to mention the odd gig siphoning tens of thousands from illegal offshore casinos or other scam artists who managed to stay out of the authorities' reach (and at which Stokes looked the other way). It made a nice balance, even if it wasn't as lucrative as a pure black hat existence. At times it made her feel patriotic, that she was returning the favor America had given her by letting her stay and go to MIT. Maybe he would someday see it the same way, too.

She set to tracing the IP address the chip was programmed to send to. But as expected the trail ran cold short of the final destination. She was able to reach back to Hong Kong, but no further. It reached the headquarters of Cathay Computer Works, but from there she could not traceroute past the firewall doing the network address translation for their private network.

A half hour later Stokes signaled that he had the NetSys executives on the Scan-U. Yvonne logged in to see his image scanning her bungalow, as if looking for Colin again. Two more holographs began to resolve, and Yvonne called up her Cyber Styletto image. Rita Sanchez and another man appeared.

"Ms. Sanchez. Good to see you again."

"Good to not see you again," Sanchez said.

"Ah, yes. Sorry about that. But you know the regulations regarding my identity." She studied the face of the man who materialized along with Sanchez. "And Liang Runnan," Yvonne said.

"Who is that? How do you know me?" he said.

"I know of you. CEO at Pebble Computer in Beijing. Put the company on the map. Then you disappeared in 1997. Rumor has it certain Chinese government officials wanted kickbacks for introductions to foreign investors and you couldn't pay."

"I assure you my departure from that company was a personal decision. I only wished to spend more time with my family."

"It didn't make sense, considering the system of extortion over there. Everybody knows to put something away for when the government comes calling. Unless it's already been extorted, so to speak."

"What are you insinuating?" Liang asked. "Who is this, please?"

Stokes cut in. "Our agent knows better than to spread unfounded gossip, doesn't she?"

"So, now you're working for Network Systems." Yvonne continued as if Stokes hadn't said a word.

"I am Senior Vice President and Director of Logistics and Manufacturing for the Pacific Rim Region," Liang said.

"Wow," Yvonne said. "That must be a big business card."

"What can we do for you, Miss…?" Liang said.

"Actually, it's what I can do for you. The source of your infiltration was a microchip, planted on the motherboard of your compromised server. The chip is controlled by an entity somewhere in China, but I haven't been able to pinpoint it yet. The signal stops in Hong Kong, just a stone's throw from Guangzhou."

"That is where the server is manufactured," Liang said. "A microchip? Are you sure?"

"All I have is the serial number. Can you tell me who made it?"

She read the number to him, and Liang searched his database, but he reported no returns. "I will launch a full investigation," he said.

"There isn't time for that," Yvonne said. "Stokes, I'm going to have to track this down the old fashioned way. I'm going to put together a team and go to Hong Kong. The only way we can take it further is to go to the data center at Cathay." She smiled over the possibility of doing the field work herself, getting out of the dark computer labs she haunted and out of reach of Stokes and the other government stiffs who'd cramped her style since the arrest and subsequent arrangement.

"Finally," Sanchez said. "Some progress."

"Of course there will be a few expenses not covered in the original agreement," Yvonne said.

"Expenses? With what we're paying you? Out of the question."

"Nothing major," Yvonne went on. "First-class airfare, luxury hotel accommodations, expense account…"

"She's only kidding," Stokes said. "And if there are any extra costs, the government will cover them."

"Oh, Rohan. Shame on you," Yvonne said. "Adding to the national debt. What would the president say?"

"Just keep the expenses to a minimum," he said.

When Sanchez and Runnan signed off, Yvonne shed her avatar to finish up with Stokes. "I will need a team, Rohan. You know I'm still a suspect for hacking the W88 caper in China, so I need some people I trust to help me. It'll be easier to remain undercover if I have the right people to work with."

"You're really willing to go back there, Yvonne? If they catch you they might put you on trial anyway, with or without proof."

"Well, you can't blame them. If I hadn't caught them with their pants down over those nuclear warhead designs, they might have invaded Taiwan. I can see why they'd be a little upset."

"Speaking of having someone's pants down, is that person I saw at your place earlier still hanging around?"

"You mean Colin? I'll be bringing him along, if that's what you want to know."

Colin called from the living room, "Road trip!"

Yes, he was a boy at heart. "Separate bedrooms, I promise," she said.

"Bring me the receipts or I won't cover the hotel."

"Rohan, darling. Jealous to the end. Listen, I'm going to call an old friend, Buck Ryan. I want him and his crew in on this."

"Ryan Repo? If he's still kicking I think it's a good idea. Get some experience involved."

"Still kicking? Buck will never retire," she said. "He has too much fun screwing with deadbeats. You ever the see the face of a corporate exec when his airplane is repossessed?"

"Can't say that I have. Buck still headquartered in San Francisco?"

"As soon as I confirm with him I'll fly there to plan how we're going to proceed. I'll call you as soon as we have it together."

Yvonne's next call was to Ryan's cell.

"Perfect timing," Buck said. "I've got a triple seven in Shenzhen that I'm snatching on the twenty-fifth. Provincial official got over his head with an Aussie bank, and we're going to give him a reverse Christmas present."

"Don't forget to leave a lump of coal in his stocking," Yvonne said.

"Ha! You know I've missed that sense of humor of yours. It'll be great to work with you again. What have you got cooking this time?"

"Buck, you're going to need to call in your muscle for this job," she said. "We're talking cyber war."

BUCK RYAN

Chapter Five

4 p.m., Thursday, offices of Ryan Repo Services, San Francisco

Buck Ryan made boxcars full of money repossessing aircraft whose buyers were in default. The glamorous sounding business, though, meant spending hours in dark and dirty locations, waiting, watching and drinking gallons of bad coffee, poised for the right opportunity to move. So when it came to spending that money, Buck made up for the rough trips by making sure his accommodations back home were designed to be luxury that rivaled a sultan's. His conference room in the Pyramid seated twenty at a table the size of a landing strip. The suite was all windows except for the interior walls, which were covered with photos of the planes Buck had snatched in his quarter century in business. Looking out, Yvonne took in views of the bay, the Golden Gate and the rest of the city.

"Impressive," Yvonne said. "This is a nice upgrade from your last office."

"Wish I spent more time here," Buck said, "but the money's out there."

"This is like an aircraft archive," Colin said as he perused the pictures. He stopped in front of a Nam-era F-4. "You fly this one too?"

"Flown them all. But the Phantom's the only one I could do barrel rolls in," Buck said.

They sat at the end of the table closest to the bridge, leaving vacant a space that resembled a small hangar.

Yvonne looked into the cavernous area and asked, "Expecting more guests?"

"I've got that muscle you asked for," Buck said, "But actually no one's sat at the other end of the table since I can remember. Guess I got a little carried away with the decorating. But I've got to spend my money someplace."

There was a barely audible knock at the door to the conference room. A shaved head poked in, apologized for the interruption and smiled.

"Come on in, boys," Buck said.

The head and its owner had to turn a little sideways to get through the door. The man was his own jumbo jet, maybe six-seven and at least three hundred pounds. How he'd managed to knock so lightly was a mystery. And speaking of boxcars, he looked like he could lift one. Colin rose, in apparent awe, to shake his hand.

"This here's Woody," Buck said. "Woody Woodman. Ex-Navy SEAL. He was over in Afghanistan when they took out bin Laden."

"Let me guess," Yvonne said. "He's the one you use to sneak up on the bad guys."

Buck laughed. "You'd be surprised," he said. "Woody is as quiet as a mouse. Until it's time to get to work. Then he's kind of like a tornado—you never know when or where he's going to hit, but when he does… well, let's say there is significant destruction."

Woody looked down, as though embarrassed by Buck's praise. He'd shielded the two men who'd entered after him, and they popped out to be seen. Buck introduced them as Luzon Boland, his security man, and Nigel Cross, his Oxford-educated lead pilot. Boland wore a cowboy hat, but took it off to bow and shake Yvonne's hand.

"A true gentleman," she said. "I like that."

Yvonne was about to ask Buck how this little man, who appeared to weigh only slightly more than she, had been named the team's security leader over Mount Woody, but when Boland slipped into his seat with the grace of a ninja she began to understand why. With a name like Luzon he had to be from the Philippines. Probably trained in the art of Eskrima or Kali.

Buck noticed her watching him. "It's why we call him Silk."

"So he can slip in and out of anywhere."

"And it feels so smooth when he does."

"And Nigel? I suppose you have a nickname too, since everyone seems to have one."

"At your service, Miss Tran," he said in regal sounding British diction. If she'd met him on the street, she would have assumed him to be a college professor. He was short and a little overweight, with the gray hair and posture of a man who's career was in books, not airplanes. "Some people call me Prince. Can't say as I know why."

"Prince Nigel," she said. "It fits."

Buck gave the boys Yvonne's background, including her "nom de net" of Cyber Styletto. Then it was time to get to work. "So, Yvonne, you've got a cyber war brewing," Buck said. "You piss off the Chinese again?"

"Not yet," she said. "But if they're up to what I suspect, it's bound to happen."

"Details."

She laid out the story of the power outage and what she knew about the mysterious chip. "The electronic trail goes cold in Hong Kong," she said. "After that all I've got is the serial number. I need to get there and track it down. If I don't, whoever's behind it can infiltrate and disable huge amounts of infrastructure with this weapon."

"More than traffic systems, I would assume," Nigel said.

"The government is spreading the word to possible buyers of servers with those chips, but who knows where they've gotten to, and how long they've been at it."

"So we've got to move fast," Buck said.

"I don't want to speed up your plans," she said, "but is there any way you can be ready to leave tomorrow?"

"Whaddya think, boys?" Buck asked.

Nigel and Silk nodded in agreement, but Woody just stared. "Well, boss," he said. "We haven't discussed terms."

"Oh, yeah. I wouldn't have made half my money if I didn't have Woody along. He keeps me focused on the bottom line."

"Not to worry," Yvonne said. "Network Systems will take care of you. I'll guarantee it."

Colin piped up. "Hey! You never said anything about money to me."

Yvonne smiled. "Darling! Isn't my delightful company enough?"

"Not if it's going to be in separate bedrooms, like you told your man, Stokes."

"Don't worry, we'll cut you in."

Buck sat back in his chair. "Stokes? You still working for that old softie?"

She folded her arms as if the question were too probing. "It's unavoidable. He still has leverage from the CIA case. If it wasn't for him I might be doing time, or worse. They might have deported me to Mother Russia."

"Well he's a lucky bastard, getting to work with you on a regular basis," Buck said. "At least we have this opportunity, and boys, let me tell you, this lady is smart enough to make Bill Gates look dumb."

"And sexy enough," Colin said.

Yvonne gave him a look that said shut up. She'd already had second thoughts about bringing him along. His piloting skills could be valuable, but his maturity and reliability under pressure were in question. More important, she didn't want her professionalism and authority brought into question. If Buck's team thought for a second that she wasn't as dedicated to the job as they were, the mission might be in jeopardy. And as long as Buck had Nigel to help fly, Colin would have to be satisfied with a backup role.

"Let's lay out our plans," Buck said.

Buck's soldiers leaned in to coordinate.

"Don't you think the team needs someone with special knowledge about the Chinese spy network? Could be important."

Yvonne raised a hand to her ear. The implant! Stokes was eavesdropping again. "Dammit, Rohan," she said. "Back off!"

The others at the table looked on in surprise as she seemed to be conversing with a ghost.

The voice came back. "Open the front door, Yvonne."

"What?"

"I'm outside."

"Outside where?"

"Buck's office."

"Oh, no," she said.

"What's wrong, honey?" Buck asked.

She drew in a breath and exhaled it slowly. "You're not going to believe this, Buck, but Stokes is here."

"Here in San Fran?"

"Here at your front door."

"Well, he'd better be delivering a pizza, otherwise I'll get rid of him," Colin said, getting out of his seat.

Buck put his hand up to stop him. "Hold on, son. Let's bring him in and see what he wants."

"You sure, boss?" Woody said.

"He's a very important man with a very long title." Buck smiled. "We'll hear him out and then get rid of him."

Woody trudged off to the office lobby. Yvonne cursed under her breath. This was the second time Stokes had embarrassed her in public. She promised herself it would be the last.

Stokes walked in with Woody behind him and stopped to introduce himself. He was not a small man, but his average stature diminished as he stood next to the giant, and he began, in Yvonne's mind, to look less like a government official and more like Woody's hand puppet. She could only hope that he hadn't come all this way to make another attempt at getting back together.

He reached into his jacket and produced a small box, which he slid into the center of the table. "The latest technology from CyberCom," he said. "These molar implants are set to communicate with each other. One for each of us. They're all on the same bandwidth, so we can use them like hidden radios. You just slip it over your molar…"

"Wait a minute," Yvonne said. "What do you mean, 'us' and 'we?'"

Stokes puffed out his chest. It was still a puny image next to Woody. "You don't think I came all this way to deliver a box of hardware, do you?" he said.

Colin spoke. "Actually, we were hoping it was pizza."

"I'm going with you," Stokes said.

Buck Ryan laughed. The rest sat in amazement.

"The hell you are," Buck said. "You old goat. You can't just horn in on this deal. Aside from these little jewels, you don't bring anything to the mission."

"Oh really? Which one of you is the expert on the Chinese intelligence structure?"

Buck looked like he was thinking it over. "It's not like we couldn't use that knowledge," he said.

"No!" Yvonne said. "He's not going. He'll just get in the way. He only wants to go to prove that he hasn't turned into a complete wuss. But it's too late for that. All those years behind a desk… and Rohan, you're putting your life in danger."

"Listen," he said. "When I worked the field for the CIA I lived with danger every day. Yeah, it's been a while, but I haven't forgotten how to take care of myself."

"And what about your wife?"

Stokes smiled. "I told her it was a secret mission. I didn't even have to lie. She was actually quite proud of me."

"Well, he might do all right," Buck said.

"Why not?" Nigel said. "He's younger than me and Buck. How badly would he do?"

"I still say no," Yvonne said. "And if you remember, this is my mission. I am making the decisions, including about personnel."

"Well, how about this…" Stokes began to pace behind the chairs, like a teacher giving a lecture. "You've been promised a lot of money for this mission, both from the government and Network Systems. If you want to see any of it, you'll find me a seat on that plane."

Yvonne could take no more. "Rohan, you've gone crazy. You're just going to walk off your job at the Pentagon to ride with us?"

"Looks like I already have," he said, folding his arms.

Yvonne could have lived without the money from this job. She still had plenty from her pre-CyberCom escapades, and thank God the government hadn't made her give it up. But Stokes also held the purse strings for her future missions, and if she wouldn't let him in on this one, who was to say if he'd hold it against her and cancel any future work? There was her lifestyle to consider, and having three homes thousands of miles from each other, plus the cars and the plane and the fashion show closets was an expensive proposition. His desk job gave him the connections necessary to keep her from working for other governments, and even some of her private sources. If she pissed him off he might go so far as to re-initiate the charges against her and tack on a few for the more clandestine operations he'd allowed. And now Buck and his team smelled the money too. They might be angry she cost them a big payday. It was like fighting the entire U.S. intelligence system. She'd lost to Stokes before when he tracked her down; she was going to have to lose this one too. But in her mind it was two strikes against him.

All six now sat around the curve of the table and waited for her decision. Stokes would be trouble. She'd have to find a way to keep him on the periphery, occupy his time with meaningless tasks that kept him away from her.

"All right," she said at last. "You can come. But if you mess things up for us we'll dump you somewhere over the Pacific."

"You'd leave me out there, all alone?" Stokes asked.

"If you want company maybe we could find an island that still had cannibals."

Stokes smiled. "I'll behave," he said. "And you'll see just what I can bring to this team."

"I can't wait," she said.

WOODY WOODMAN

MGM GRAND MACAU

Chapter Six

7 a.m., Sunday, San Francisco International Airport

Stokes turned right, down a cramped aisle into the coach section of Air Asia charter flight 711, a non-stop to Macau packed with people eager to try their luck at the MGM. Yvonne smirked as he shook his head over the seat he'd been assigned, in the middle of the last row. He wouldn't even be able to lean back during the ten-hour flight with the bulkhead behind him. He turned to make sure she was following him, and saw she was not.

"Where are you going?" he asked.

She smiled. "First class, of course."

Buck, Woody and the others all headed left, holding in their laughter. "Them too?" Stokes said.

"We always fly up front."

He took the crumpled boarding pass and waved it at her. "Then what am I doing with this?"

"Rohan, darling. I tried. But by the time I knew you were coming it was too late to get you a first class seat," she said.

He turned to go back to the gulag of the last row, then stopped. "Wait a minute," he said. "When I showed up, you hadn't even made your plans for this trip. You just did this to spite me."

The queue of passengers loading up behind Stokes as he blocked the aisle began to get restless. An old woman pushed her carryon into his leg. She blurted something in Chinese. He didn't know the words, but Yvonne could see he understood her meaning as he dropped his head and started walking back.

In Macao the group had to wait almost a half hour for Stokes to disembark, since literally everyone else on board was in front of him. Yvonne had considered leaving for the hotel without him, but he'd only track her down through her cochlear implant, and she was getting tired of that. He came up the tunnel looking as though he'd been flying in a laundry hamper—his jacket and shirt were wrinkled, and one pant leg had risen high enough to show a stretch of bare shin above his sock, and was held in place by static cling.

"You get into a fight back there, Stokes?" Colin said.

"I think I was stuck between two sumo wrestlers," he said.

Maybe the rough treatment had been too much. Yvonne hadn't anticipated his seatmates being Woody's size. "Sorry," she said. "I got a little carried away with the joke."

"I had it coming," Stokes said. "I put you on the spot back in San Fran."

"And a few other places," she said.

A stretch limo met them outside the terminal to take them to the MGM. "Pansy Po," Yvonne explained as they got in. "We're old friends. I told her we were coming."

"Nice to have friends like that," Nigel said.

"Listen," Yvonne said. "Pansy will show us a great time tonight while we get ready for the job. But you need to promise not to win too much at the tables. It kind of makes her mad if she thinks she's paying at both ends. Just think of it as another way to handle the bill."

Silk smiled at her. "You don't have to worry," he said.

"Why not?"

"Three decks, shuffled every other hand,'" Buck said. "Silk had to stop counting cards after most of the houses changed their strategy. He was one of the best blackjack counters in the business before he joined our team."

"Father taught me in Manila," Silk said. "I clean up there too."

"Now he just bets the animals," Woody said.

Stokes looked up. "Animals?"

"Horses, dogs… the occasional rooster."

"That's where big money is anyway," Silk said. "Better odds."

"Your father was Doug Boland, wasn't he?" Stokes asked.

"Yes. You know him?"

"Knew him in Iraq during Desert Storm," Stokes said. "Tank man. One of the few to fight there and in Nam. Toughest son of a bitch I ever met."

"Met Lu at Doug's funeral," Buck said. "We brought him on a couple of years after, when I saw him win a martial arts tournament in Thailand."

"Sorry to hear that your dad passed away," Stokes said. " He was the last of a breed, if you ask me."

While Stokes cemented his relationship to Buck and the rest of the team, Yvonne pulled out her laptop and started typing. There was a Chinese spy satellite in synchronous orbit over Hong Kong from which she might be able to get images from the airport. The warehouse that stored Network Systems computers assembled in China was nearby, and if she could locate it, they could create a map of how best to execute both her mission and Buck's simultaneously.

The limo quieted as she worked. "No," she said. "Keep talking. Don't let me kill the conversation because I have some work to catch up on." She nodded towards the driver. Pansy Po may trust him, but Yvonne could not afford that luxury. In Macau, she knew, everyone had a price—even Pansy's driver could be working both sides.

The others traded more gambling and war stories while she hacked away. Finding a signal from the satellite was the easy part— she knew from experience what wavelengths the Chinese—and most other sovereignties—used regularly. But what encryption keys might be employed this week were anyone's guess. She launched a search program, but it might take some time to unlock it—her laptop was nowhere near as powerful as the computers in her lab, and it crunched the numbers like it. She might have to continue the process in the hotel room, which was riskier, since the longer it took to complete the task, the better the chance her activity might show up on People's Liberation Army security agency scans. A stationary target was easier to locate.

Stokes saw what she was doing and leaned in. He whispered, "CyberCom intelligence says they're using one of the Jinzhong protocols. You might narrow your search there."

She switched to CyberCom's private communications channel and accessed a secret folder. It listed protocols intelligence had uncovered in the previous month. She typed in a few more commands to go in that direction. Within a minute the program had given her access to the satellite's output and functionality. It was currently relaying images from a military installation in Taiwan. "The bastards," Stokes said. "That's a violation of international sovereignty." He smiled at Yvonne, to acknowledge that she'd be doing the same thing.

Yvonne changed the coordinates to position the camera to Hong Kong International and the satellite responded. "I can't do this for very long before they realize what's going on. Maybe just a few seconds," she said. "So I'm gong to have to take get wide angle shots. As long as we can blow them up later, they'll be fine."

"This is the first time I've ever hoped their resolution was as good as ours," Stokes said.

She downloaded images for fifteen seconds, and then disconnected the link. "Glad we were able to do that while we were moving. I hope it's enough to tell us what we need."

"If not we can always take a taxi together and try again."

Yvonne rolled her eyes at Stokes to let him know it was another nice try that wasn't going to work.

Pansy met them at the hotel. Thanks to her history in the casino Yvonne was given a million dollar limit at the tables. Each of the men was allowed fifty thousand, plus bar privileges, which made them visibly happy. For accommodations, the men were doubled up in ground floor villas. Buck and Nigel volunteered to room together in what they called the "seniors suite." "You know how early we elders have to get to bed," Nigel joked.

Colin and Silk, being the youngest, paired off. "Great," Colin said. "There's an Armageddon Squadron tournament I can play in while we're here."

That left Stokes and Woody. Stokes took another look at the big man and said, "If there's only one bed in that room I'm in a lot of trouble."

Yvonne was given a penthouse. She and Pansy dismissed the rest of the crew, and went off for a brief tour, and then to the owner's private office. If Buck had missed anything in decorating his place back in San Francisco, Pansy had it here… and more. The furniture, she explained, was all handcrafted. Hardwoods from South America, Macael marble from the quarries in Spain. Yvonne sat in a Reitveld chair and sipped a twenty two-year single malt. Pansy sat and draped her hands, heavy with jewels, over the arms of her chair. Against the royal backdrop, she looked something like an empress from one of the dynasties. It was not too far from the truth—she and her family had created a new ruling class, even among the supposed socialism of the Chinese state.

"You're quite the host," Yvonne said. "I feel guilty coming here to ask for a special favor."

"I always show my friends the best times. Besides, I am still in your debt for saving the casino's network. Anyone else and I'm sure we would have been hacked by gangsters. What I spend to entertain you and your friends is just a fraction of what that would have cost me."

"In that case," Yvonne said, sipping her Scotch, "I need a few things for that project I mentioned in my message. You still have your munitions connections, I assume."

"In this business, I have to," she said. "But I thought you didn't like guns."

"I don't. But this job has some special risks. I don't always go on location to do my work. I usually snoop long distance, where the bad guys can't touch me."

"Something here in Macao?"

Yvonne explained the logistics of her search. "We landed here first because I have to sneak into Hong Kong. I may still be on their list of suspects wanted for questioning. Besides, I needed someone I could trust to help with this equipment."

"Got your shopping list?"

"A van, for starters," Yvonne said. "With the logo of the Cathay Computer Works on the side. And then some weapons—enough for six."

"I can get you some Uzi-Pro. They have a polymer pistol grip. Your boys will love them. I'll see about some explosives too."

"Oh, I don't think we'll need that."

"You better take them along. And I'll see you get some night vision goggles. Best to poke around when it's dark."

"Are you sure?"

"You computer nerds are all alike," Pansy said. "Never think about the physical danger. You're lucky you have me on your side, Yvonne. Brains and beauty—we still make a good team."

"Wait a minute," Yvonne said. "Brains and beauty? What's left for you?"

Pansy laughed and hugged her. "You have brightened my week," she said. "I'll make sure everything is waiting for you when you get to Hong Kong. But now, come on, let's have some fun before you have to leave."

They started for the casino when Pansy stopped and put her hand on Yvonne's shoulder. "Speaking of special risks, there's one more thing you should know."

Yvonne lifted an eyebrow.

"Shi is in Hong Kong too," Pansy said.

"Does he know I'm coming?"

"No. But I wanted you to be on guard. Ever since Hong Kong went back to China he's had a thing for harassing foreigners there. His men are always looking to make trouble. You show up with your team and someone's sure to notice."

"Thanks. I'll have the boys split up on the ferry so we're not so obvious."

They walked into the casino and paused to survey the action. Yvonne looked for the team members, but Pansy stopped and fixed her gaze on Colin, who was trying his luck on the slots.

"Yours?" she asked.

"Just a plaything."

"May I borrow?"

Yvonne led Pansy over and introduced her.

"Having any luck?" Pansy asked him.

"Not a bit. These things aren't rigged, are they?'

"Totally fair," she said. "But slots is for children. Come with me and I'll show you an adult game."

"Like…?"

"We'll start with baccarat. After that, who knows?"

Colin shot a look at Yvonne, as though he might offend her by going off with Pansy. Instead she wanted to thank her friend again, but to say it in front of him would be rude. "I don't mind at all. Go ahead," she said. "Get yourself an education."

Pansy winked at her, confirming that the young man would no doubt learn a few things in the course of the evening.

In the morning the team met in Yvonne's suite to go over photos of the airport. "We've had our fun, gentlemen," Buck told them, "but now it's time to prove we deserve the big money. This mission is going to be tougher than usual. Not only do we have to avoid the usual airport security, but our repo target is connected to the government, and has his own people. We don't know whether they'll be in proximity when we move to take the Boeing, so we're going to have to do recon before we can move in. It's one thing to take a plane from a corporate hangar. Taking one from a member of the Chinese government is something else."

"This has international incident written all over it," Stokes said. "Any connection to U.S. government operations would be a disaster for CyberCom and NSA."

"That means you have to stay as far in the background as possible, Stokes," Buck said.

"And then there's my little project," Yvonne said. "I need to get into the Network Systems warehouse and examine a few of their servers to determine if this is where the Mandarin chip is being added."

"Exactly. We need to coordinate all this."

Yvonne spread satellite photos that Pansy had printed for her over the coffee table. The resolution was not as sharp as she had hoped, owing to the small window of time she had to download them before Chinese authorities caught on to her activities. The Network Systems warehouse was in among a block of industrial buildings in a remote area. It was at least a half mile from the hangar that housed the 777, and she could not be sure which structure, exactly, was the one she sought.

"So it's not going to be easy," Buck said. "Our best plan is to recon the warehouse and the jet during the day, and make our move in the wee hours. Woody can go with Yvonne for protection, and we'll take Colin to compensate."

When they were done with the preliminary logistics, Yvonne slipped the photos into her briefcase. "Pansy tells me Hong Kong is crawling with Chinese intelligence these days. We're going to have to be extra careful."

"Shi Tao?" Stokes asked.

"Yes. My old friend from MIT."

"And my counterpart in espionage at PLA. It's hard to believe he learned everything he knows in America, and then took it back to China to work against us."

"The American way," Colin said. "Give our enemies access to our secrets and then act surprised when they use it."

"I've always had a thing for him," Stokes said. "Maybe we'll get to finally meet."

Yvonne held her emotions inside. She'd had a thing for Shi when they were back at MIT, too. He'd been as smart as she when it came to computer theory. And he'd been able to hide his motives the entire time they were together.

"Listen," she said. "When we land in the city we have to split up. We can't just have six American commandos…" She looked at Stokes. "Make that five… walking down the street together."

"Best let me go by myself," Silk said. "I blend in better than the rest of you."

Yvonne wasn't sure. He was only half Asian, and the half that was his father seemed pretty obvious. But Buck had said Silk knew how to hide himself, and she trusted that opinion.

She and Colin would pretend to be a couple again. Buck would pass as her dad, Nigel as his.

That left Stokes and Woody to team up. Woody looked Stokes over like he was choosing a ripe tomato. He paused, took a deep breath, and said, "You think people will really believe you're my bitch?"

Everyone broke up, except for Stokes.

When the meeting was over Yvonne decided to disguise herself before the ferry to Hong Kong. She wanted no part of Shi Tao. Their time together had been difficult. He was jealous, vindictive, and a nightmare of competitiveness. Even when they were dating he made every class assignment a personal battle between them to see who was better at writing and hacking code. It was because of him she almost gave up her career before it started.

It wasn't even a class assignment, but a dare. Yvonne boasted she could infiltrate secure systems faster than he, so he made her prove it. The elevators in the Langham Hotel had just been converted to a computer system that had improved their efficiency thirty-five percent. It had been in the Globe. The system figured out how long it would take each car to respond to a call, and sent the one that would get there first.

"We'll screw them up," he said. "Take the whole system down." He was more malicious than she had imagined. But she couldn't resist the competition. She had to beat him. She decided she would get in, send a car or two to the wrong floor, and get out. No one would even realize she'd done it.

They raced to see who could hack in first. They sat, brazenly, in the lobby and typed away. "I'm in!" she said, just a moment before he said the same thing. The next step was to prove she had affected the system. But in her rush to win she forgot her plan to divert the cars—there just wasn't time. Instead she simply pulled the plug on the entire system. As did Shi. They both yelled, "Done!" at the same time.

They laughed and pushed at each other playfully. No one could tell who had actually reached the system controller first, so this one would have to be declared a tie. But Yvonne stopped laughing right away. Paramedics had been called to the lobby. There were people trapped in the elevators. "Don't worry," Shi said, "they'll figure it out in plenty of time."

Except that one of the people on an elevator was an old man who had suffered an attack of angina. His wife was bringing him down to meet the medics. Now they were in between floors. Yvonne could almost hear her screams for help into the emergency phone.

By the time the hotel techs were able to access the car and reach the couple, the old man had gone into cardiac arrest. He died on the way to the hospital.

Maybe if they hadn't been playing with the system he would have made it. Maybe Shi had been the one to pull the system's plug. Did any of that matter? She knew it didn't.

Shi couldn't care less. "His number was up," he said when he learned what happened. For him, it was all about being on top, no matter who got in the way. They didn't see each other after that; didn't even speak again until graduation. And since then she had promised herself—no violence, nothing that could inflict anything more than financial harm.

Knowing Shi, he'd given her picture to every security agent under his command, and she'd be picked up the minute she showed her face. She had to do something about that.

She took her hair and fixed it into a ponytail, then stuffed it under a coolie hat she bought the night before, after she'd met with Pansy. She chose her most unremarkable outfit from the clothes she'd brought—baggy jeans and a tan blouse—and added a large pair of tourist sunglasses. Still she was afraid it was not enough. Someone would recognize her. Most of her missions had been conducted in the safety of cyber space. This time she'd have no firewall to protect her.

A knock on the door startled her. Stokes said he'd left his pen on the table.

When she let him in it was his turn to laugh. "Who are you supposed to be?" he asked. "A refugee from a Charlie Chan movie?"

But when she admitted her fears about being seen, he softened. "Here," he said, opening one of her suitcases. "Let's see if we can do something about that look." He found her makeup kit and opened it, over her protest.

"Relax," he said. "You forget I was in the field for years as part of my CIA career. I had to learn a few tricks to keep from being spotted."

He knelt in front of her and applied powders and mascara. He took her hair from the ponytail, grabbed a hair brush and restyled her. Yvonne felt the gentleness of his hands as he worked; his touch was soft, the way she remembered.

When he was done and she looked in the mirror, she saw a completely different woman—a tourist from America, somewhere in the Midwest—not exactly a look she'd ever thought of achieving, but a far cry from the Uygur province.

"I'd still go with the sunglasses, though," he said. "Just to be sure."

"You should do something about your appearance, too," she said.

"Very funny."

"I'm serious. Shi must know who you are. It would be quite a coup for him to have you in custody."

He reached into his jacket pocket and pulled out a fake mustache. It was more of a small caterpillar placed between the nose and upper lip, an Inspector Clouseau getup that made Yvonne laugh as he adjusted the corners. Stokes wasn't so bad after all. If only he hadn't been married.

She reached to grab her bags for the ferry trip, but Stokes beat her to it. "Can't let you hurt those magic hands," he said as he headed for the elevator. "Those fingers may just save us from the next cyber attack."

PANSY PO

Chapter Seven

Monday, December 24, Peninsula Suite, The Peninsula Hotel, Hong Kong

Stokes showed the team how to attach the implants to their molars and demonstrated their operation. "A simple bite at the back of the mouth, like you're eating a cracker, turns it on," he said. "Another bite turns it off."

Silk sat back in one of the luxurious chairs in Yvonne's suite, looked out towards Victoria Harbour view and grinned. "And what happens at dinner? On, off, on, off, every time you take a bite?"

"Doesn't work that way. As long as your molars don't make contact it won't change the setting."

When the group was satisfied the hardware worked, they split up. Buck and his team, except for Woody, dressed in Cathay Computer Works uniforms, took the van and headed for the airport to do recon for the night's mission. They took Colin and Stokes with them, although Stokes wouldn't be allowed out of the van. Woody stayed with Yvonne. They hadn't been able to get a uniform in size XXXXL, and didn't want to attract undue attention by trying to have one custom-made at any of the tailors in town. He'd have to work in the background when the team went on its mission.

It was just as well. Yvonne could use him to run interference. She needed to get to Asiaworld-Expo, the convention center a few minutes from the airport. Cathay had a shop there where visitors could purchase smart phones and laptops, and the demo models tied into CCW's network. If she could get close enough, she'd be able to access the company's database and finally ping the IP address that had launched the cyber attack on Silicon Valley. But getting that close was a problem. She couldn't just stand in public and run a program to infiltrate the CCW server.

She transferred a worm she'd written to access the server from her laptop to her smart phone. It was a new model they'd surely have in stock. If she could switch her phone with one of the displays, it might look like she was just playing with the functions while deciding whether to buy, instead of hacking Chinese intelligence.

A salesman met them before Woody was even finished walking through the doorway. He was a skinny kid, maybe as big around as one of Woody's legs, but what he lacked in size he made up for in aggressiveness. "I know what you need," he said in English. "Great deal on iPad today. Beat any other store in Expo. You buy today, take back to America tomorrow."

At least Yvonne's disguise was working. The salesman assumed they were a tourist couple on the prowl for cheap electronics. She played along. "What do you think, dear," she said in her best midwestern accent. "The kids already have iPads, but maybe we should get one for the dog."

"Oh, I don't know, honey," Woody said. "He might have trouble using his paws on the screen."

"Hmmm," she said. "I guess it's not bowser friendly."

Woody groaned at the bad pun.

Although the salesman didn't speak English very well, Yvonne could see he knew he was being put on. But he didn't leave them. Must be working on commission, this one. She pointed towards the center of the store, where the smart phones were on display. "But I will take a look at one of those," she said.

"Excellent choice," the salesman said. "We have latest of everything in stock."

She walked slowly, looking at several of the models, making sure the salesman didn't get suspicious. She picked one up and examined it as though it were incomprehensible to her. "I don't even know how to turn it on," she said.

The salesman rushed in to help, but she put it back and grabbed a pink device from the rack. "Well, this one's a pretty color. What does it do?"

"Many functions for hardworking American family woman. Hundreds of apps."

"Sounds too complicated for me."

"Then we have this simple model here. Entry level so not confusing."

"But I don't like the color," Yvonne said. "Don't you have something pretty and simple too?"

She had the poor kid on the run. Time for Woody to go into action. All he needed to do was turn sideways, and he knocked a stand full of accessories to the ground, and ear buds and belts and cases in plastic, theft proof packages scattered over the shop's carpet. "Oh, I'm sorry, sir," Woody said. "Seems like I'm always doing this when I go shopping. That's why my wife hardly ever takes me."

The salesman began scooping merchandise from the floor. Woody leaned in, ostensibly to help, and knocked his shoulder, sending him sprawling. This was Yvonne's cue.

She went straight to a display of Blackberry phones. Woody helped the salesman to his feet, but made sure he was facing away from Yvonne. She found the model she owned, unlocked it from its tether with a key Silk had given her, and replaced it with the one she'd programmed earlier, pocketing the store model. Woody continued to "help" the salesman, brushing his clothes off, fixing his collar and piling loose accessories into his arms, making sure he stayed occupied. Yvonne had to smile while her new "husband" gave her the time she needed.

She connected through the store's private router to Cathay's in-house network and let the worm dig into the company's database files. Once linked, she contacted the Network Systems server back in Key West and had it power cycle to phone home. While the chip on the motherboard sent out its signal, she monitored the packet capsule logs to determine where the chip's commands originated.

This time a ping traced past the Hong Kong data center and back out of China. To Japan and then to South Korea. From there it jumped to Bombay. Next, over the border with Pakistan into Lahore. She watched as the signal made its way around the hemisphere. It knew no politics, respected no governments. It was a tool of man, yet more free in this respect than any human being.

Finally the signal terminated in Puli Khumri, on the back side of the Hindu Kush in Afghanistan. Maybe a hundred miles from Kabul.

Woody watched over her shoulder as the signal resolved on the tiny map. He whispered, "Fuck. Al Qaeda country."

"You know it?"

"I did a year there with the SEALS."

"I thought you guys only worked in water," she said.

"Think of it as a sea of sand," he said. "You can still drown in it."

The salesman was finally regaining his bearings. He still smelled sale. "Ah yes," he said. "You have found best of smart phones. Special price today."

"No need to talk it up," Yvonne said. "I'll take this one."

The salesman acted as though it had been his easiest sale of the day. "Wonderful. Excellent. I get sales slip. Need your information."

"Oh, no, no, sir. I'll pay cash." Yvonne pulled a roll from her purse and peeled enough hundreds from it to cover the cost of the phone, a warranty plan and a hefty commission for the young man. "No need to write this one up," she said. "And we'll keep this our little secret… right?"

"Highly irregular…" The salesman started to protest, but when he counted the bills she handed to him, he quickly changed his mind.

They turned to leave while he tried to interest them in more electronics.

"Expensive little phone you got there," Woody said as they walked through the mall. "Especially considering you already owned it when you went in."

"The price of doing business. Besides, I'll just add the expense to the bill I give Stokes." She pulled the new phone from her pocket and gave it to Woody. "A little gift for being such a good actor back there," she said.

They stopped at a coffee shop and sat at one of the tables lined up outside. "So now we know where the attack originated," Woody said. "What do we do now?"

"A good question. Depends on what we find in the warehouse tonight." She was about to go on, but felt something—an electronic pulse—at the back of her jaw. The molar implant. It was connecting to her surgically augmented hearing—the cochlear implant—and producing a signal like she'd never experienced before—part sound, part feel, almost like a dentist's drill originating from her jaw. She jerked her head back and looked around.

"Something wrong?" Woody asked.

"I don't know. I have this weird sensation."

"Lots of women get that around me."

"No joking, Woody." She felt the outside of her jaw. "I think we're being monitored somehow."

Woody didn't move, but she could see his eyes darting about the mall. "Can you localize it?" he asked.

"I wish I could. But it's like it's coming from inside my head. The only person who's been able to do that is Stokes."

This didn't seem like one of his tricks. He would have communicated to her by now. Besides, he was with Buck and the others at the airport. They'd be too busy avoiding security. This had to be someone else. But even that didn't make sense. She must have left her molar implant on by mistake—accidentally tapped her teeth together. Damn the technology. Even so, Stokes had assured them the implants included a jamming component to preclude being tracked. She resolved to remove the implant as soon as she got back to the hotel.

The sensation stopped as abruptly as it started. "Let's get out of here," she said.

As soon as the elevator let them off, Yvonne noticed the door to her suite was open slightly. There was no cart in the hallway, so this was no housekeeping call. Woody ran ahead of her and positioned himself to throw the door wide on her signal.

But from inside, a familiar voice. "No need to be violent. Do come in."

The big man eased the door open. Shi Tao was lounging on the sofa, his feet up as though relaxing after a hard day. He was engrossed in Yvonne's laptop, and was busy poking around the keyboard, although he seemed frustrated, obviously confused by her login protocol. Two of his agents rummaged through drawers and luggage behind him. Shi had helped himself to the bar and had a martini on the table next to him. Very dry, Yvonne recalled. Woody tensed, ready to rumble.

"You Americans are always so ready to become physical," Shi said. "A country of super comic book heroes, or at least you imagine yourselves to be. I see you've grown to be just like them, Yvonne. And what is this disguise? Trying to hide your secret identity? Shame on you."

"Woody, this is Shi Tao," Yvonne said. "Chief of Blue Army in the People's Liberation Army." She took off her sunglasses and hat, and shook her hair free.

"Much better, Yvonne," Shi said. "This is the beauty I remember. And so much more beautiful in person than the cheap Cyber Styletto avatar you use."

"Liberation Army?" Woody asked. "Talk about oxymorons…"

Shi ignored him. "Do not forget, I am also master at Shandong Jinan Lanxiang Vestibule School."

"I've heard of that one," Woody said. "A school for training computer spies."

Yvonne folded her arms. "Not like other schools. Instead of Reading, Writing and Arithmetic, students major in Denial of Service, Trojan Horses and Worm Coding."

"We've got the three R's, and they've got the three wrongs," Woody said.

Shi turned his palms up, offering them the pose of someone who had been insulted for no reason. "I am merely a poor soul, risen through hard work from a lowly American college student to prominence in his homeland." He'd kept his dark good looks from those days too. He was her age, but still looked thirty.

"More like cheating and bribery than hard work," Yvonne said. "An unbroken record of lies at MIT." She quietly tapped her molars together to activate the implant again.

"Statements made in earnest, I assure you. How others misinterpret them is another affair."

That was you in the mall, spying on us."

"Honestly, Yvonne. You come to Hong Kong, access a secret government satellite, steal from an innocent electronics salesman, and are planning who knows what else… Who is spying on whom? I can have you arrested for any of those things."

"Try proving it," Woody said. "And we paid for the smart phone."

"Do you have a bill of sale?"

Woody tapped his sledgehammer of a fist into his palm. Yvonne put her hand on his bicep to calm him.

"My dear Mr. Woodman." Shi gulped down the last of his martini, swung his legs off the sofa and faced them. "How little you understand about Chinese law. My suspicions are proof enough to keep you in custody for several weeks, maybe months. And just think of the embarrassment and trouble you will cause your government.

Give me the phone and I will forget that charge. As for the others, we are still investigating."

Woody handed him the smart phone.

Shi's agents came up from the back rooms and reported to him in Chinese. It sounded as though they'd found nothing else. He closed the laptop and stood. "Thank you for the refreshment. And I will keep this, as a memento of our good times together."

Woody tensed again. If she let him, he could probably handle this trio, whether they were armed or not. But for sure there were more agents in the lobby or outside. It would be best to cut their losses and let him have it.

The agents waited for Shi at the door. He stopped in front of Yvonne and took her hand, brought it to his lips and kissed it. "Still so lovely," he said. "Seeing you again has awakened the erotic memories of our affair."

"I'm sure the sex was all that mattered to you," she said.

"You underestimate me, my dear. I had other uses for our love as well." He nodded at Woody and went out. His agents trailed him, walking backwards to make sure Woody didn't follow. Yvonne watched as they got into the elevator.

"I need a drink," she said as she pulled her smart phone from her pocket.

Woody headed for the bar. "Are you sure it's safe to call Buck now? They probably bugged us while they were searching the suite."

"I'm glad he didn't confiscate this." She pressed a few buttons, waited a second, then pressed a few more. "Actually, I'm calling my laptop. A little program I installed a while ago just for moments like these."

"High explosives?"

She laughed. "Maybe Shi is right. Maybe we are all about violence." She pressed one more button and put the phone back. "Just a simple hard drive routine. By the time Shi hits the front door the disk will be wiped clean."

"Too bad," Woody said. "A little violence might be just the thing to get Shi's attention, not to mention the Chinese."

"I'll keep that in mind. We may need it later. If they're watching us tonight's operation is in jeopardy—both aspects."

"We've been watched before on jobs like this," Woody said. "Buck's pretty good at stealth. But we will have to be careful. We'll need a decoy of some kind."

"You know, every day goes by I'm more glad we brought Stokes along. I'm sure he'll help us create a suitable diversion." She put two fingers into her mouth and reached in the back, and began working the molar implant free. It took a minute of wrenching, but she pulled it out and laid it on the bar. "We'll have to take a look at these, too. So far it's caused more trouble than it's saved us. I switched on while Shi was here, but no one seems to have heard."

"Right." Woody dropped his arm, wound up, and belted himself across the jaw with a right cross. He spit his implant out and it clattered onto the counter.

"Nice," she said. "I'm sure that's how Shi tracked us down today."

"Yeah, but how did he know about the satellite? We didn't even have the implants working then."

"He couldn't have pinpointed my signal that fast. Someone had to have told him we were on our way here and he was waiting for that kind of activity."

"Who knew?"

She rattled off the list. "A couple of execs from Network Systems, and Stokes. Maybe he mentioned it to someone on his staff back in D.C."

"And your friend Pansy. You sure you can trust her?"

Yvonne sat on a stool to think about it. She'd known Pansy for years. They'd been business associates, then good friends. But time and politics made people change. Shi had managed to hide his real motives for years. Maybe Pansy had too. But then, she'd warned her about Shi being here. The relationships were becoming more complicated by the minute. How much easier it was to stay in her lab and do her work remotely.

Woody brought her a vodka stinger. He drank a beer straight from the bottle. "So what are you going to do without your laptop?"

"Looks like I'm going to need another favor from our friend, Buck. I've got a lab in Paihia Beach. If I can get back there I've got the equipment I need to bring the Afghani operation down. Once we pick up the repo do you think Buck would mind making a little detour on his way to Sydney? Say, a quick stop in Auckland?"

SHI TAO

NIGEL CROSS

Chapter Eight

3 a.m., Christmas Morning, Hong Kong International Airport

Tonight's sortie was an old-fashioned stakeout, Buck had said. If Yvonne had ever been on one, she would have understood his sentiment, but instead she was anxious, feeling exposed to dangers she never experienced working in her labs behind the protection of computer screens and miles, sometimes thousands of them, between her and her adversaries. "The way it ought to be," he said, "No fancy technology, just hardware and guts." The team had removed their molar implants to keep from being tracked by Shi's men. They would operate tonight in true secret, using nothing that emitted a signal, nothing that could be monitored or traced. All movements would be synchronized. Communication would be by sight alone. The others on Buck's team were wary. They were used to their devices.

"Trust me," Buck said. "This is the way we used to do it. It'll be more fun than any job you've ever been on."

Yvonne wasn't so sure. For the first time in her cyber career she was hacking in person—infiltrating an operation like a human version of the viruses she unleashed on bad guys, dressed in a gray Cathay Computer Works jumpsuit instead of one of her thousand-dollar outfits, and wearing a simple pair of tennis shoes—no stilettos tonight. She was crouched behind a beam on a catwalk, waiting for a signal from Woody that the way was clear and she could advance a few more feet towards the rogue servers stored below on the warehouse floor.

She remembered what she'd said to Stokes about his being a desk jockey. Despite the wars she fought in cyber space, she had to admit she'd been one too. The driving and flying she did at the threshold of danger, the hang gliding and base jumping—all those risks were mitigated by the right equipment and dozens of safety procedures. They were exhilarating, yes, but nothing like facing real, live people, who might, by the way, try to kill her.

Stokes had worked for years in the field before he settled into a plush leather chair. And he didn't flinch when the team asked him to run the diversion that would keep the Chinese security forces off their backs for the duration of this mission... they hoped. Right now he was touring Hong Kong with Pansy's limo driver, dropping the molar implants at sensitive locations—Cathay Computer Works corporate headquarters, Hong Kong Telecom, Hang Seng, a branch of the Bank of China, even the precinct security building near their hotel. He would turn the receivers on before planting them outside each office, and occasionally voice instructions over the set frequency. With luck the Chinese would think an operation was under way, and would dedicate their forces at these locations, instead of the airport. Yvonne was glad she'd never told Shi about her enhanced hearing during their affair. If it hadn't been for that, she'd never have figured out how his men had found her.

The plan was for she and Woody to swing by the hotel once they'd completed their part of the mission and pick up Stokes. The trio would then rendezvous with the rest of the team in time to repo the Boeing. But that was only theory. As they slipped around one corner after another trying to find the servers, she knew they were falling behind schedule. Too late and they'd have to head straight for the hangar where Buck and the boys were working to circumvent the jumbo owner's own security men and free the plane for return to Sydney.

Stokes might be stranded in Hong Kong. And if they left him behind he'd eventually be at the mercy of Shi, who would be furious over the break-in here and the theft of the aircraft. Yet he took the risk. "If anyone gets caught," he'd said, "it's best if it's me. Washington won't let me stew in a Chinese prison for too long. They'd negotiate a trade for a Chinese spy. Any of you, they might let you rot for months."

It sounded right, but as Yvonne worked it over, she realized Stokes's value to the Chinese had other implications. His stay in a cell might be brief, but it would be horrific. Whatever time Shi had with Stokes would be spent trying to break him, get him to spill what he knew about U.S. intelligence. She regretted the whole idea now. She could have asked Colin or Silk to drop off the implants and kept Stokes in the background, where he belonged. But when she proposed the idea, he jumped at it. She thought it had something to do with his never-ending efforts to impress her enough to restart their affair, but she realized now that he was doing it to ensure the success of the team.

Woody gave her the signal to move forward. He made no noise as he moved along the catwalks. His SEAL training allowed him to become a specter at will.

Around the next corner they found the servers. They looked down at what was essentially an assembly line of espionage. A series of Network Systems servers lay in a row on a long metal table. Some were in crates, others had their covers removed and sat exposed under the fluorescent lighting. Still others waited their turn for techno surgery.

At each of the open boxes a technician in a CCW jumpsuit leaned in to scan the labels, and remove the foam lining and other packaging. She watched as one of them removed the server's cover to get at the motherboard. The man donned surgeon's loupes and carefully soldered in an extra microchip. He replaced the board and hooked the server up to a laptop to check its operation. When he was satisfied with the performance of the chip, he replaced the packaging and applied new labels and tamper-proof seals to the box, and handed the unit off to be stored in an aluminum shipping bin.

The whole process took less than twenty minutes. At that rate the Chinese could manufacture enough bogus servers to give them access to control systems throughout the U.S., as well as Europe.

When she crept alongside Woody, he whispered. "Time to do your thing. Just remember, if anything goes wrong, I'll be right behind you."

He pulled the end of a black fiber line from a case on his belt and held a stirrup open. Yvonne slipped her foot into it. She felt like a child's toy as Woody picked her up and eased her over the railing. Then he let her go into a silent, controlled descent to the warehouse floor. She stepped out of the line, gave a tug and let it recoil back into the case.

He had dropped her behind a girder. She would step out and walk towards the techs as though she had come through the front door.

Yvonne reminded herself that the key was to act as though she belonged there. It's all attitude, Nigel had said. "Back during the Falklands War, I convinced an Argentine guard that I'd gone to university in Buenos Aires. He let me pass into a top secret base so I could get a look at their fighter capabilities."

She hadn't used her Chinese in a while. The others had laughed as she practiced phrases on the drive to the airport, asking herself questions and providing answers. But it was necessary. There'd be no opportunity to correct herself if she said something wrong.

She walked smartly to the man who appeared to be in charge, a rather dull looking fellow with heavy glasses and a mop of greasy hair. His CCW logo was circled in red to indicate his authority. She introduced herself as " Píng," from the Beijing office. He would never get the joke. She said she was there because several servers delivered to companies in the U.S. had failed to yield full access to systems, and she had been assigned to observe procedures.

The supervisor looked her over. He checked the photo she'd stitched above the CCW logo on her jumpsuit, then smiled. "Why don't we go to my office," he said. "I have complete records of every machine that has passed through here."

"No, no," she said. "I must observe the operations as they occur."

"Are you sure? Also I have some very nice brandy. Imported from France."

This jerk was hitting on her? She supposed it was better to have this than his suspicions about her identity. But she'd have to keep him interested in her and not her mission. "Delightful," she said. "Let me first observe for a few minutes and I will be happy to join you."

The man clapped his hands together. He pointed to a room with a window that overlooked the proceedings. "I will be waiting for you there. Don't take too long!"

Really. He was planning on doing her right in front of the other employees? He *was* a jerk. She considered calling in Woody to break him in half. But the mission came first.

She watched the techs work, strolling from station to station, looking over their shoulders. After a few moments she stopped behind a woman. "You see?" she shouted. "Look at this shoddy work! This chip will never function correctly."

The tech turned to face her. "There is nothing wrong. What are you talking about?"

"You have attached the chip in the wrong place. This is the work of an amateur," Yvonne said.

The woman looked at her coworkers. "I have made no mistakes," she said. As she turned, Yvonne unclipped the ground wire that connected the woman's wrist to the table.

"And you are not properly grounded," Yvonne said. "The procedure calls for you to be tethered at all times."

She called to the supervisor. "Wang! Come here!"

He was the last thing Yvonne needed. She had to work fast or she'd be forced to call in Woody, and things would get pretty messy.

She grabbed the motherboard off the workstation. "Give that to me. I must file a full report," she said. She slipped the board into the pants pocket of her suit.

Wang walked back from his office, the bottle of brandy dangling from his hand. "What is the problem?" he asked the tech. "This is an important representative of the parent company. How dare you argue with her. If she says the work is incompetent then it must be."

He must be desperate for a woman. He didn't ask to see the work, just took her word for it. "Come," he said. "Let us talk about it in my office."

If she went in there she'd be trapped. But if she ran now they would catch her. Yvonne walked towards Wang's office, desperate for an option.

A loud metal crash echoed from the far side of the warehouse. Wang and the workers all looked in that direction. Then another, sounding like a bulldozer had run into the steel racks where equipment was stored. "Someone is there!" Wang shouted.

No kidding, Yvonne thought.

Two of the workers already had machine guns. Wang took one of the weapons and led the charge. "Quickly! Whoever it is must not escape." The noises continued as most of the techs pursued this phantom trespasser.

Then, something rattled on the cement floor at her feet. A lug nut. Did someone throw it?

She looked up. Of course! Woody was leaning over the catwalk railing, unfurling the fiber line and waving her over. Yvonne ran to the spot while the remaining techs watched, slipped her foot into the stirrup and let Woody pull her up. She waved goodbye to their open-mouthed stares.

"It was you back there making that racket," she said as he lifted her over the rail.

"The supervisor didn't look like your type."

"Yes. He should have known I prefer vodka."

By the time the techs realized what was happening and called for Wang and his men to return, Yvonne and Woody were back outside. They raced to the CCW van. Yvonne drove, and sped towards the Boeing's hangar to join up with Buck and the others.

"Wait a minute," Woody said. "I thought we were supposed to pick up Stokes."

"I know, I know. But there's not enough time. We spent over an hour at the warehouse. Buck's probably ready to leave by now. If we go back for Rohan that puts four men in jeopardy."

"You'd just leave him?"

She hated making this decision. "He knew the risks," she said.

Woody looked in the side view mirror. "Um, Yvonne?"

"Yes?"

"I was just going to tell you to slow down so we don't attract attention…"

"Right," she said. "Good idea."

"But it's too late now. We've got a security cop on our tail. Better speed up instead."

She floored the accelerator and got the van up to ninety, but couldn't shake the cop, who hit his lights and siren. As they came within sight of the hangar, Woody signaled her to stop, and she slammed on the brakes until the van skidded close to the side of a small brick building. Yvonne got out to meet the cop, who pulled his service revolver.

Yvonne flashed her best smile while Woody circled around the far side of the panel truck. A few minutes ago she didn't want to seem sexy, now she was counting on it. The guard lowered his gun.

"Emergency repair job," she said in Chinese. "There's a flight waiting to take off and I have to repair the Flight Control System computer."

"No flights scheduled to leave at this hour," the guard said. "First flight six a.m." He brought his gun back up.

Yvonne switched back to English. "That's what you think," she said, just as Woody whipped a fist into the man's temple, knocking him out.

"He probably called that in," he said. "We've got to get that jumbo off the ground now!"

They got back in and drove the last few hundred yards to the hangar. Yvonne could see Nigel in the pilot's seat, with Colin as co-pilot. Looked like they'd been ready to go for some time. They ran up the steps and dove inside. Buck and Silk toasted them with a shout of "well done!" They'd even had time to raid the bar. But as soon as they saw it was just the two of them, they asked about Stokes.

"We all agreed to the plan," Yvonne said. "Stokes did too."

"The man has guts," Buck said, lifting his glass again. "I hope he'll be all right." But there was no time to lament the decision. He signaled the others to get the plane under way.

Woody heaved the entire stair assembly away from the fuselage and slammed the door shut, but the top of the steps was still higher than the wing. "What are we going to do about that?" Yvonne asked.

"Only one thing to do," Nigel called from the cockpit. He started the turbines. "I'll have to nudge it as we clear the hangar. If I'm careful I can push it out of the way without damaging us."

The engines roared to life. A few more checks on the gauges and Nigel was ready to push off.

"Wait!" Colin yelled. "There's a car pulling up in front of the plane."

"Damn," Woody said. "We didn't want to tell you. We ran into a cop on the way. He must have called it in before we could take care of him."

"That's no cop," Nigel said.

The team pushed into the cockpit to look out the front windows. A red vehicle idled near the nose gear.

"What is that?" Colin said.

Buck leaned over the throttles to get a better look. "It's a ... a taxi?"

The rear door to the car swung open and a man started to get out, then leaned back in to give the driver a tip and pick up a briefcase. He waved the driver off and turned to face the aircraft.

Stokes.

"What the…" Colin said.

"Well, open the damn door," Yvonne said.

Stokes ran up the steps but stopped at the top. Woody had pushed them a good six feet from the plane's doorway.

"Wait," Stokes said. "I'll run back down and push them closer."

"We don't have time for that," Woody said. "Besides, I don't think you can do it. They're a little heavy."

"Then what should I do?"

The sound of more sirens was just audible over the whine of the engines. More security was on the way. "You've only got one choice now," Woody said.

"What if I don't make it?"

"That's why they bring me on these trips," Woody said. "I won't let you miss."

Stokes tossed his case to Woody, then bent at the knees and swung his arms to practice. He straightened and swung his right leg as though preparing to use it to fling himself across the gap. He tried the bent knee pose again.

"Will you make up your mind and come on?" Woody shouted. "The cops are getting closer!"

But it wasn't cops. In the distance they could see several vehicles approaching. Even in the dark they could tell the military had been alerted.

Buck yelled at Nigel, "Move this bucket! Now!"

The engines revved and the plane began to move.

"It's now or never, Stokes," Woody said. "You didn't come all this way to be left at the station."

Stokes bent low. From behind Woody, Yvonne could see he'd closed his eyes. He pushed off, throwing his arms into a swan dive.

She could see his jump was short. He was going to crash to the concrete thirty feet below.

… had it not been for Woody, that is. The giant reached out and caught Stokes by the wrists, and pulled him into the cabin with a biceps curl.

"Wow!" Stokes said. "You ever want to join a trapeze act, I'll be your reference."

The jumbo eased into the Hong Kong night. As Nigel had predicted, the stairs rolled with the plane's motion until they were outside the hangar. Then he turned to knock them over, out of the path of the wing landing gear. As soon as they fell away he went to quarter throttle towards the runway. But the military was gaining on them. Woody grabbed an Uzi from one of the bags and headed for the still open door.

"Better idea," Silk said. "Use this."

He held open a bag with some bulbous-looking metal balls. "M67 grenade," he said. Blow some holes in tarmac and chase is over."

"Right," Woody said. "Let's link up!"

Silk took two grenades from the bag and stood in the doorway. The plane was moving sixty or seventy miles an hour now, and the wind was almost louder than the engines. Woody took hold of Silk's waistband, and with his other hand braced against the doorframe. He leaned out and held onto Silk as the smaller man braced his foot against Woody's thigh, extending himself a good six feet past the door, where he could get a clear look at the pursuers.

"Excellent view," Silk shouted. He ripped the pin from the first grenade and flung it over the wing. As he threw the second, the first exploded. Yvonne caught on to the idea. She began tossing grenades to Silk, who pulled the pins and let them fly past the fuselage. "Good thing Pansy suggested these," Yvonne said.

The explosions sounded like thunder behind the jet. But no one could see the damage except Silk.

"Are they doing the job? Did they stop the trucks?" Yvonne had to know.

Silk signaled Woody it was okay to pull him in. When he was back inside, he closed the door and walked to his seat, picked up his drink like nothing had happened. He crossed his legs in front of him and took a swallow. "They won't be using this taxiway for quite a while," he said.

Nigel steered the jet towards the main runway. "Watch this, lad," he said to Colin. "Just in case the Chinese get a whim to follow us."

Four Chinese J-10 jet fighters sat on the tarmac under harsh white lights. Nigel eased the Boeing to the edge of the concrete, until the plane's wing extended well out, far enough so that Colin could see the winglet at the end would hit the fighters.

"Are you sure about this?" he said.

"I've been wanting to try it for a long time," Nigel said. "I may never have this chance again."

Nigel gave the jumbo a touch more throttle. The wings began to lift. Workers near the fighters scrambled for cover. The Boeing's winglet caught the canopy of the first plane, smashing the polycarbonate into millions of granules. Colin abandoned his co-pilot seat to press against the side window for a better view. Nigel kept the Boeing steady and wielded the winglet like a sword, slicing through the canopies of the remaining three jets. "There," he said. "Four wickets without a break. They call that a double hat-trick where I come from."

"No more time to waste, Nige," Buck called.

Nigel turned the nose onto the runway and went full throttle. The Boeing was in the air in thirty seconds, and out over the South China Sea in minutes. The team could finally relax.

Yvonne sat next to Stokes. "Rohan, what happened?" she said. "I mean, how did you know not to wait for us?"

"When the limo dropped me back at the hotel and you weren't there to meet me, I knew you'd run out of time," he said. "I kind of figured that would happen. So I had a backup plan."

"Pretty smart," she said. "Glad you made it. I wasn't relishing the idea of leaving you to wait for Shi."

"He might have been a little rough once he found out who I was."

He grabbed the briefcase he'd brought and opened it. "I had a chance to do some shopping before I made my rounds. I thought you'd like to have this. It is Christmas, if you remember." He handed Yvonne a new MacBook. "Sorry I didn't have a chance to wrap it."

"Rohan, you darling," she said. "Well, since it's Christmas, I have something for you, too." She reached into the pocket of her jumpsuit and gave him the motherboard from the CCW warehouse. "We make the connection between CCW and the Chinese government, this could prove that the chip that hacked the NetSys server was installed with their knowledge."

"Ah, just what I always wanted," he said. "Thank you, Yvonne."

SILK BOLAND

Chapter Nine

5 a.m., Christmas Morning, over the South China Sea

The team wasted no time finding the goodies the provincial official had stashed in the 777. The cabin had been completely customized to his order, with three full bars spaced throughout, and a full kitchen at the tail. While the others sampled the high-end liquor, even bringing soft drinks to Colin and Nigel in the cockpit, Silk busied himself—to his teammates' surprise—in the galley. He'd found a case of jumbo shrimp on ice, and was preparing a peanut sauce to go with them.

"Never suspected you could cook, son," Buck said. "Your dad's idea of fine dining was cold pizza and warm beer."

"My mother love to cook, and he love to eat. Maybe that's why they marry."

"Guess I'll have to raise the level of cuisine I provide you boys back at the office."

"Yes. Been meaning to talk to you about that."

The aircraft was all first class, a fact that didn't escape Stokes's notice. "Let's see you stick me in coach now," he said as he dipped a finger into Silk's creation for a taste.

Nigel came back from the controls to get another drink, leaving Colin up front. Buck turned to Yvonne. "Has your friend ever piloted a jet this size?" he asked.

"It's all right, chief," Nigel said. "The boy's got the knack. Give him a few more minutes and he'll have us doing barrel rolls."

While the rest of them indulged in the jumbo's luxuries, Yvonne looked up from her new computer. "Buck, I need to ask another favor."

"Anything, Yvonne."

"Would you mind if we detoured to Auckland so I can get to my lab before you deliver this plane? The job's not done."

"Umm, anything but that."

"You don't understand. I haven't geolocated the source of the network attack yet. Stopping these guys is a matter of national security."

"How would I explain it to my client? I can't just take a hundred-million dollar jet on a joyride. I promised them it would be safe and sound in their hangar by the twenty-sixth."

She tried her sexy smile on him. "That still gives you a few hours."

"Extra thousand miles, chief," Nigel said. "Each way. Not sure we can make it with the fuel we have on board. The Chinese ground crew hadn't filled it yet. Cutting it too close if you ask me."

"If we land in Sydney, it'll take me a full day to get to my lab," she said. "I'm not sure we have that much time to waste."

Stokes cut in on her behalf. "Yvonne's right. Now that the Chinese know we're on to them, they might make a move. We have to keep pursuing until we know exactly where the cyber attack was issued."

"We'll have to find a place to top up, you know," Nigel said. Can't just pull up to the pumps at Auckland. And we'll need clearance to land, too. Flight plan is filed for Sydney."

"Yvonne, can you contact my office back in Washington?" Stokes said. "If I can get through to CyberCom, they'll arrange everything."

"You see?" Yvonne said. "I told you it was a good idea to bring Rohan along."

Buck agreed to the detour, providing Stokes's office provided confirmation for the change in plans, something he could show his client to justify the delay. While he went up front with Nigel to plot the course change, Yvonne went back to her laptop.

"WiFi is working, but I can't link up with my equipment in Paihia," she said when prodded. "Having some trouble locating the IP." She opened the Skype application.

"Calling the Geek Squad?" Stokes quipped.

"My neighbor. Just want to make sure everything is okay."

The friend answered on the first ring. "Was just about to try you, Yvonne," he said. "Something's happened. Someone's broken into your place. I'm with the police right now."

"Bruce! Did they get anything?"

"Yvonne, you never told me you were some kind of computer wizard," Bruce said. "The police say there's all kinds of cables and monitors in your office. You running a porn ring?"

"What? No," she said.

"Whatever else you had in that room is gone. Stolen. Middle of the night, must have been. No one heard a thing."

Stokes was trying to listen in, but looked frustrated, since he couldn't hear the other end of the conversation. Yvonne thanked her neighbor and said she'd get back to speak with the police as soon as she could—but it might be a couple of days. She turned to Stokes and Buck.

"Shi Tao. It has to be. I keep some of my equipment running while I'm away so I can use it remotely. I accessed it from my suite. He must have used the logs at the hotel and traced the connection to my condo."

"This is getting personal," Stokes said.

"You have no idea, Rohan. I'm going to make him sorry for this."

"And no chance you can wipe the hard drives by now."

"They've already pulled the boxes apart and copied them. Once they decrypt they'll have everything—my programs, encryption keys, and records of my communications. I've got backups, but they're useless as long as Shi has them too. I'm starting from scratch."

"We'd better put out an advisory ASAP. Anyone with sensitive information that might be on your computers. You can be sure Shi will have his agents trying to hack into it. What about your other labs?"

Yvonne tried to access her equipment in Key West and Long Island, but her efforts got nowhere. "They're down," she said. "Shi's people are already in."

Woody turned from the window. "Hey boss?"

"Hang on a minute, Woody," Buck said. "Yvonne has a crisis."

"We all do."

"Hmm? What's wrong?"

Just as the big man started to speak, Colin called from the cockpit. "Need you up here, Buck. ASAP."

"The Chinese may not have liked what we did to their tarmac and aircraft," Woody said. He pointed out the starboard window to two J-10 Chinese "Annihilator" fighters shadowing the 777. There were two more off the port side.

Buck ran into the cockpit. The others crammed up against the windows.

One of the Chinese pilots pulled within a hundred feet of the fuselage, close enough for everyone to see when he pointed at the jumbo and then at the ground.

Woody said, "If he thinks were turning back, he can go…"

"How far are we from Hong Kong?" Buck asked.

"About five hundred miles," Nigel said. "You thinking of making a run for it, chief?"

"Could we screw with them long enough to make it to a friendly airport?"

"Closest one is probably Manila. About a half hour away at this speed."

Buck crossed his arms. Perhaps if it were only his team on board he might risk it. He looked over at Yvonne and Stokes. "I can't take a chance with you two. Unfortunately you're too important. We piss these fighters off and one of them is liable to fire a missile our way."

"If we're important, then we're too important to allow to fall into their hands," Stokes said. "Don't worry about making us comfortable. Throttle up and show these guys what a 777 can really do."

"Smile back, Colin," Buck said. "Give them a thumbs up like we're going to do what they want."

Colin followed instructions, but only until his hand fell below the bottom of the window frame. Then he switched from thumb to middle finger.

"Easy, son," Buck said. "Let's make them think we're following orders." He turned to Nigel. "Nige, make your turn long and lazy. We're going to loop at least fifty miles south. If we can lull them into buying it, we'll break off and try to hit Philippine air space before they recover."

Silk had come up from the galley when the commotion started. "Get us out of this, boss, and I have my mother meet us and cook a real dinner for you."

Yvonne was still trying to get through to CyberCom on her laptop, but the Chinese were jamming to keep the jumbo from calling for help. She tried a series of frequencies that Stokes gave her, but the Chinese were on to them, further proof of Shi's capabilities, and a warning to Stokes that CyberCom communications might be compromised. But he had another idea.

"Think you can hack that spy satellite again, Yvonne?"

"Sure. But why?"

"They're jamming our frequencies, but they'd never think to jam one of their own. If we can get in, maybe we can relay a message to CyberCom before they catch on."

Yvonne turned her head slowly to look at Stokes. This was not the soft executive she'd had an affair with three years ago, nor the paper pusher who handed out assignments and sucked up to his Pentagon superiors. He was in the field again and thriving in it. It was the part of espionage he loved and in which he belonged. Sure, maybe he'd latched on to this mission because he still had feelings for her, but as the case unfolded he'd become more and more involved in the work, and left the dreams of romance on the sidelines. And strangely, this turned her on more than any of his awkward advances.

"Rohan, darling, did I ever tell you you're a genius?" she said.

"No. You only said I was great in bed."

So much for her new assessment. She looked around to make sure no one else had heard his comment. She'd slept with him, with Colin and Shi. She'd rather none of them knew about the other affairs in her private life.

Although her original laptop was gone, she remembered enough of the protocol to access the satellite within a few minutes. Stokes dictated an emergency message directed to Admiral Lucas at CyberCom, and she fed it into the satellite's onboard computer, redirecting it to broadcast back down in a frequency that would reach the offices in Washington D.C. As soon as it was sent she shut the link down, before the Chinese noticed.

"The Ronald Reagan is patrolling off Palawan. If we can get word to them we might get some help. But for now it's sit back and pray that the Pentagon folks are not all at some holiday party, getting blitzed," Stokes said.

"Somebody has to be on duty at CyberCom." Yvonne said.

"Usually it's me," he said. "Now that I'm away who knows who's minding the store."

Nigel banked the aircraft in an elongated arc across the South China Sea. He rolled the plane to a steep angle, to make the jet pilots think the jumbo was coming about, but kept the yaw to a minimum, allowing the plane to drift much further south, towards the Philippines, than the turn should allow. But after a minute the lead pilot caught on to the tactic. He pulled his jet within sight of the cockpit again and pointed towards the mainland with a series of hard gestures.

"Looks like he's getting impatient," Nigel said. "Time to make our move, I'd say."

Buck turned to face the team. "This is going to be risky," he said. "We can't outrun them, so we're relying on surprise. If we don't hit Philippine air space in a couple of minutes, the Chinese will probably start firing on us. I suggest buckling up."

Silk clicked himself into his seat, but it was clear he was upset about the developments. "Damn," he said. "Peanut sauce almost ready. Now go to waste."

"Don't worry, my friend," Woody said. "Now that we know you can cook I'm sure there'll be plenty of opportunities."

When everyone was strapped in, Nigel rolled the jumbo ninety degrees from port to starboard, and nosed down hard, sending the Boeing into a dive like a World War II fighter on a strafing run. The g-force of the move sent pots and pans flying in the kitchen, and cinched the midsections of the passengers. He kept the engines at full thrust, and the resulting descent was stronger than gravity, lifting everyone slightly from their seats.

The move caught the Chinese off guard, as hoped, and gave the team a head start of about ten miles. They were traveling close to the speed of sound now, beyond the plane's limits, and the fuselage began to shudder from the turbulence. "Keep it up, Nige!" Buck yelled, "A few more minutes and we'll lose 'em."

The ocean flew up towards them. "I'm going to have to pull up before we hit, chief. It'll slow us down," Nigel said.

He eased back on the controls to level off a thousand feet above the water. The tactic and the increased air pressure at low altitude slowed them, and gave the Chinese a chance to close. The J-10s were capable of almost three times the speed of the 777, and the jumbo's lead disappeared in seconds.

Lights from the islands were barely visible on the horizon. "Of course, there's no guarantee they'll just stop when they get to the Philippine boundary," Buck said.

"Thanks for reminding me, chief." Nigel brought the Boeing to full throttle again, but the four Chinese jets kept pace. Instead of ringing the aircraft as they had done before, they kept a mile or so behind. "I think you know what that means," he said.

"They're locking on to us," Colin said.

As soon as he said it, a deafening sound, like a jackhammer on steroids, echoed from the tail section. Nigel grabbed the control column tightly as the plane yawed, and managed to hold it straight, but it was clear something had been damaged.

"Cannon fire," Buck said. "They targeted a spot that would hurt us, but not kill us. He leaned in between Nigel and Colin. "That's it, boys. No sense pushing this any further. Bring the plane around and let's head back to Hong Kong."

Nigel eased the plane into a tight arc to show the Chinese there would be no more trouble, and put it on course for their origin. The J-10s formed a diamond around them: one in the lead, two at the sides and one trailing. They traveled with their escorts like that for a few minutes, but as quickly as the formation had been formed, it broke apart—the fighters each scrambled in a different direction, leaving the jumbo on its own again. Scanning the horizon from their side windows, the team saw why—a squadron of fighters was approaching from the south. Six planes bore down on the scene. As they passed by they could see they were F-22s, no doubt from the carrier. The American planes took off after the J-10s, driving them out of sight within a minute.

A message from a Colonel Martin popped up on Yvonne's laptop. "That's Lucas's adjunct," Stokes said. "He must have gotten our call."

Stokes read it aloud. "Sir. Sorry for the delay. Took a few minutes to authenticate your transmission. We don't get many messages from Chinese satellites."

Woody laughed and slapped Stokes on the back, sending him across the aisle.

"Ouch! That's a fine reward for me saving our butts," Stokes said.

"We're not completely out of the woods yet," Yvonne said. "We've still got to track down the source of the cyber probe. You know Shi isn't going to wait to make his next move."

"Can you do it from here?" Stokes asked.

"I need my lab and more bandwidth than this plane carries. And Shi made sure it's not available."

"No way we can get you back to Key West for at least a couple of days. By then they might have launched another attack."

Yvonne slumped in her seat. "I can't believe I left myself so vulnerable. If only I could get my hands on some new equipment."

Stokes nudged in next to her. "Go online. I want to Google something," he said.

When she brought up the web page he opened to a map of the region and studied it. After a few seconds he said, "There's only one place within flying distance where they have that kind of hardware," he said. He put his finger on it.

Yvonne looked at him as though he was joking. "Afghanistan?"

"Bagram Air Base. I know the commander."

"Stokes, are you sure?"

"You said the signal originated from near there. I'm going to put you right next door. When you ping them now it'll come back loud enough to knock your earphones off."

They got up and headed for the cockpit. Just one more detail to take care of. Yvonne poked her head in to see Buck helping Nigel and Colin navigate back towards Sydney. She used her helpless little girl voice this time. "Buck?"

Buck turned around.

"You don't really want to go to Sydney, do you?"

GENERAL MAGADAN

Chapter Ten

11 a.m., Christmas Morning, on approach to Bagram Air Base

The approach to Bagram was as uneventful as a landing at a commercial airport, which, after the bronco ride the team had experienced out of Hong Kong, caught them by surprise. Conversation on board the 777 stopped for a few seconds as the plane circled in from the south, passing eight miles high over Karachi and the Pakistani frontier. Who knew if the skies would be clear, or if terrorists on the ground had the means to launch missiles at the jet and its American cargo? What if the Iranians were patrolling nearby and decided to take some pot shots? Or maybe the Pakistanis themselves, those experts at duplicity, felt like taking them down? Yvonne held her breath as they crossed over from the Arabian Sea.

It was Buck who broke the silence and the mood when he reminded everyone that this wasn't an American jet. It still bore the logo and colors of the People's Republic of China.

Yvonne imagined clusters of mujahedeen below, gazing up at the big bird through their binoculars and wondering what the hell a Chinese jet was doing up there, but figuring they'd let it pass because they weren't at war with that country. In fact, with China and the United States competing over philosophies and economics, they probably applauded its arrival. For the team, the jet's normal appearance was better than camouflage.

General Cyrus Diaz-Magadan met them as they disembarked. He had a warm embrace for Stokes, and added a huge smile when he was introduced to Yvonne. "We don't get too many visitors here," he said. "And we hardly ever get beautiful women in person. You're a rare combination, Miss Tran."

Yvonne was taken back at the general's blunt remarks. It wasn't unusual for a man to come on to her when they first met, but she expected a man of such high rank to maintain some formality, especially with the rest of the team within earshot.

Stokes explained. "You'll have to excuse Mags. He's been on remote assignment for the last four years. Being without a good-looking woman for so long sometimes makes a man say exactly what's on his mind."

Magadan was a small man, shorter even than Yvonne, but more than twice as wide, and had the hard look of someone who'd been born into a tough neighborhood and had to fight to get anywhere in life. He proved Stokes's point further. "At least when I ran the installation in Thailand I could buy a little recreation for myself once in a while. But in this hellhole, the best-looking things are the villagers' goats."

So he wasn't politically correct. In fact, he wasn't even fit for mixed company. But they would only have to be there for a day or two before they could isolate the elusive IP that had haunted Yvonne ever since Key West. She was excited just being there, on the tarmac—she was close now, close to solving the mystery of the rogue microchips, and so physically close to their source she could almost feel it. Stokes had been right about coming here. He was proving to be right about many things.

After a few minutes back at the commander's office, which had been decked out in non-denominational holiday ornaments, as was much of the base, they were assigned billeting and given a quick rundown of the layout of the place, where they could go and where they couldn't. Magadan kidnapped Stokes for a catch-up session in his private quarters nearby, which he promised contained a full bar. He invited Yvonne along too, ostensibly for some "Christmas cheer," but she declined. The team would get the grand tour later, after they'd had a chance to relax from their seven hours in the air.

Back in her room—a cinder block cell of about twelve feet square—Yvonne tried to use the internet to continue her search, but couldn't get on. When she inquired she was told access was extremely limited owing to the base's sensitive operations and its proximity to enemy operations. She knew she could hack in, but decided against it—someone would notice. After stowing her gear, she wanted to do anything but sit. She found Colin outside the guest quarters and snagged him for a stroll. He was more than eager to go, and they walked out past the buildings to a place where they could watch F-22s performing touch and go landings in the desert haze. The mission hadn't been quite what he planned, he said, in the lulls between the roar of the jets. Despite the jokes at the start about them staying in separate rooms, he'd expected she would have at least spent some time with him. "After Key West I thought we had something going," he said. "But you've ignored me since San Fran."

"You know I'm not looking for anything more than good times," she said. "Besides, there's too much difference in our ages, darling. In a little while you'd realize how big that difference is."

He looked up as a C-17 lumbered in on a far runway. "We're not as far apart as you think, Yvonne."

"And what about Macao?" she said. "You didn't seem that interested in me when you went off with Pansy."

"Actually, I was hoping you'd be jealous."

So Armageddon Squadron wasn't the only game Colin played. But if he thought jumping into bed with her friend would bother her, he had some growing up to do. For now she added him to her list of men who hung on way too long after the fling was over. She supposed he was looking at her in the perverse way so many of her younger men did—part lover, and, ugh, part mother. Maybe it should have been flattering they could look at her with such respect for her matriarchal qualities, but really it was just creepy. What was wrong with them? What had happened to the James Bond type—the love-'em-and-leave-'em Casanova who went through scores of the opposite sex without a second thought? That kind of man seemed to be disappearing, at least among Americans. She supposed she, and probably plenty of other confident women, were usurping that role from them.

Yvonne knew that Stokes had come on the mission with the same hope as Colin. She was thankful he'd been seduced by the excitement of being in the field again. Maybe she could find a purpose for Colin on this mission, something to keep him engaged and occupied.

They'd walked a circle around the area of the base that hadn't been restricted, and found themselves near the general's quarters. Yvonne suggested they join the commander and Stokes after all. At least two of them would be trying to impress her, and she had an idea Stokes would join in once the competition started. It would be like watching bull moose in combat during the mating season, and she could amuse herself for a while with the show.

But Stokes and Magadan were on their way out as she got to the door. "Ah. Miss Tran," the general said. "I see you've come to your senses and are ready to join us."

"It's a small base, general. We've already run out of things to see."

"Well, I was just about to give Rohan here the insider's view. Some of the technology here is pure Star Wars. We'll have dinner after, and I'll show you that military life doesn't necessarily mean mess hall fare."

"Excellent," she said. "And maybe somewhere in that tour your technology can help us. I'm sure Rohan has filled you in on our mission."

"Definitely. We should definitely help each other out." He flashed a smile at Yvonne, revealing a set of tobacco-stained teeth.

Magadan had a jeep brought around and relieved the driver so he could lead the tour himself. He cruised the flightline, where fighters and transports were in a hive of constant motion. "Can't just let them sit on the tarmac," Magadan said. He pointed to the nearby mountains. "This is Taliban country. They'd be sitting ducks."

But the real attraction, particularly for Yvonne, was the war room, a subterranean command center bunkered a hundred feet underground. The room was a maze of computer equipment and monitors, manned by both officers and enlisted men who looked more like they were executing stock trades than prosecuting military action. She and Colin were engrossed in the work of the drone pilots.

They stood behind three of them who were sitting in a row in front of a bank of huge monitors. Each man used a modified joystick to control a Predator or a Reaper as it cruised over the desert.

"This," Colin said, "is bitchin'. "You've come a long way since I flew these babies."

Yvonne could see him doing a job like this. It wasn't so different from the games he played back at her bungalow.

"We get feeds from three satellites, including GPS, and we monitor every transmission in a hundred-mile radius. It's all coordinated in the ISR computer," the general said. "That lets us keep tabs on the movements of the potential bad guys in the region. If we can confirm that they're on our kill list, we send the drones in."

If she could tap into those feeds, Yvonne would be able not just to locate the source of the cyber attack, she might be able to see exactly who was behind it. She was eager to get to the task.

"And it keeps our need for personnel to a minimum," Stokes said.

Magadan said, "When the bulk of the forces were recalled from Afghanistan, the Pentagon stepped up our efforts here. We are literally the only thing keeping the Taliban from retaking control of the country."

"Yvonne, didn't you have something to do with the design of these systems?" Stokes asked.

"A small part," she said. The general seemed impressed, but that was all she would say about her role.

"Mind if I give those drones a try?" Colin said.

"Try 'em? I shouldn't even let you see 'em," Magadan said. "Sorry son."

Yvonne spoke up. "Then how about letting me tap into your satellite feeds so I can get a look at who we're after?"

"Can't let you do that either. You don't have the clearance."

Yvonne wondered how he was going to provide the help he promised if he wouldn't let them use the equipment. She didn't trust the base personnel to do it—compared to her they were amateurs. Perhaps she'd find a way to convince him over dinner. Stokes nodded at her as if to say he'd take care of it, but she wanted it now. She was tired of waiting for the government to go through its never-ending hoops. The days when she made her own decisions and then took action seemed so long ago now.

She made sure to sit next to the general when he hosted the team at a special table for the Christmas meal. The Air Force had flown in enough turkeys for the entire base to enjoy, and Magadan tapped into his personal cache of wine for himself and his guests.

"You're right, general," Yvonne said. "This meal is much better than I anticipated. You really do run a four-star operation."

Stokes lifted his glass in a toast. "Not bad for a one-star general," he said.

"Just a matter of time, Rohan. I'm on the short list for that second star."

"And you deserve it," Yvonne said. She traced the rim of her glass with her finger and gave Magadan a seductive look. "A man in control of this much power… they should forget about two stars and skip you up to four."

Magadan downed the rest of his glass of wine in a single gulp. "I like the way you think, Yvonne," he said.

"And I'll bet you have so many medals and honors you've run out of room and have to display some of them in the bedroom."

The general looked surprised for a second. He put down his glass and stared at her, then said, "Well, of course, there's only one way to find that out."

Colin and Stokes both looked amazed at this exchange. In fact, every man on the team seemed taken by it to some degree, except for Silk, who continued to enjoy his meal as though nothing had been said. Her sexual nature was common knowledge among those who knew her, and the term "cougar" was often applied in gossipy conversations, so why she was interested in this arrogant, fifty-something toad of a man was a puzzle.

And as predicted, both Colin and Stokes tried to assert themselves in the discussion. Stokes noted the importance of CyberCom in the nation's affairs, and Colin played the youth angle, trying to switch the talk to motorcycles, and when that failed to work, the obvious lack of nightlife at the base. But Yvonne kept playing to the general, enticing him into finding some time the two of them could be alone, although he didn't need any encouragement.

Indeed, Magadan had a wall full of honors and military memorabilia. He also had a huge computer setup that he described as "linked into every communication that goes in or out of this base."

"I am so into technology, darling," Yvonne said, asking for a demonstration. She lined herself up behind Magadan and massaged his thick shoulders. As he logged in she leaned over and licked his ear, and made sure to memorize each keystroke as he did so. She feigned interest as the general showed off his ability to access the various security cameras stationed around the base, even in the private offices and quarters of his administrative staff. They didn't reveal much of anything on this Christmas night.

"Pretty boring out there," she said.

"The real excitement is in here," Magadan said, reaching around to grab her hand. He pulled her onto his lap and put his arms around her waist. "Enough technology. Time for primal instincts to take over."

"Not so fast mon general," Yvonne said. She tried to wriggle free from his grip, but he had her held tightly.

"As you might have guessed, I'm not into teasing," he said. He stood up from the chair with her still in his arms.

"Aren't you at least going to let me get comfortable?"

"Yvonne, I'm comfortable enough for both of us." He carried her into his bedroom. It was no surprise that there were almost as many pictures and honors on the walls there as outside.

"You should at least let me do a strip for you."

He put her down, but kept hold of her wrist, and looked at her. "All right," he said. "Let's see what you can do." He jumped onto the bed and shimmied up until his back was against the headboard. Then he unzipped himself. "Show time," he said.

Yvonne loosened her belt and let it slide slowly around her waist until it came free. She looped it around Magadan's neck like a lasso and pulled his head towards hers, but broke off the move just as their lips came close.

He huffed like a frustrated elk. "No teasing. Remember?"

"But a really good tease heightens the pleasure," she said, and undid the top two buttons of her blouse.

She began to dance, to sway in the sultry way she did when she was really attracted to a man, moving her hips in little circles, raising her arms over her head as she did. She watched as his hand went deeper into the opening in his pants. Thank goodness he wasn't close enough to grind himself against her. She undid two more buttons.

"Faster," he said. "Let's get those clothes off you."

She slid her blouse down until it was around her shoulders and did a few more turns around the room.

Magadan got up from the bed. "Too long. This is taking too long." He cornered Yvonne and pinned her against the wall, grabbing her hips and pulling them into his.

"Don't you want the full performance?" she said.

"I've had enough previews. Time for the main event." He picked her up again and headed for the bed. As he dumped her onto the mattress, there was a loud banging at his front door. "What the... I told them not to bother me tonight," he said.

The general tucked himself back in and went to see what the problem was. It gave Yvonne time to put her clothes back together.

Silk smiled when the door opened. "Ms. Tran, Mr. Stokes need to see you right away. Emergency message from CyberCom."

"What bullshit is this?" Magadan said.

"I'd better go see what it is," she said, squeezing past him.

"I know what it is. He wants you for himself. I could see it in his eyes at dinner."

"Oh no, general. There's nothing between Rohan and me. I'm sure this message is legitimate."

"You tell your boy I want to see him in the morning," Magadan said. "We're going to have a little discussion about friendship."

Yvonne and Silk were a hundred feet away before Magadan finished closing his door, but they didn't slow their pace. "I thought you had forgotten," she said.

Silk looked at his watch. "Right on time. Nine forty-five. Just like you say."

"Time moves so slowly when you're trapped with a creep like that," she said.

"You get what you need?"

"Down to the last keystroke."

FARRIS MAHMUD

Chapter Eleven

Midnight, December 26, Bagram Air Force Base

Yvonne worked well into the night, using the general's account to gain the access she needed. She had the IP location in Puli Khumri, but for all she could tell it might be emanating from a house, a hut or even a cave. Without more detailed information she could still only guess. She worked two channels simultaneously, one attempting to locate and access the GPS satellite Magadan had mentioned, and one hooked up to a sex chat line to make it look as though the general was working off his frustrations, just in case someone was interested in snooping on the electronic chatter.

She stayed online until past midnight, bleary-eyed from lack of sleep, searching for activity from the IP address. She began to imagine herself back in Key West, in Finnegan's, among her bar friends and having no trouble making it to last call. What time was it back there, anyway? She'd been moving so quickly around the globe there was no telling what shape her biological clock was in. All she knew was that she needed sleep. Stokes and Buck and the others were probably all catching up on their rest. But she couldn't stop, not with knowing the answer to this mystery was so close.

After two a.m. she started to nod off in front of the laptop. As she shook herself awake one more time, she saw a signal from the IP.

Someone was reaching out into cyber space in a heavily encrypted signal.

Yvonne snapped into full alert, and began to look for a key that would give her access to what was being transferred. There was the handshake from the other side. She pinged it back to Hong Kong and knew she was on to something important. And then a third signal joined in, this one from Moscow. The amount of bandwidth in use made her certain this was a video exchange. If she could only crack the key, she would be able to see who was involved.

She worked frantically for ten minutes, knowing that she was missing her chance, and that the transmission would likely end soon. It had to be Shi on the Hong Kong end. Finally she recognized the protocol and modified her search. Images began to resolve on her screen—three men—and she divided her monitor to assign each of the originating transmissions to a third of the area. There was Shi, another martini in hand and looking very smug about himself. A young woman leaned into the shot for a moment and he pushed her aside. The bastard was probably showing off for his associates.

The second was wearing thick glasses and the robes of a cleric. Although the image was fuzzy, she recognized him immediately. Ten years was not enough to make her forget Farris Mahmud. But what was he doing here, instead of Saudi Arabia? And why the terrorist clothing and the beard? When she knew him he always wore a suit.

The third man was using a lens that distorted his appearance. He spoke French—a language convenient to all of them for the communication—with a heavy Russian accent that sounded familiar to her, and was wearing a medal that looked like the Order of Glory above the pocket of his suit. Perhaps this man had just come from a state function. As the man moved to take a sip of a drink, he turned slightly, and the image became, for a moment, clearer. But how could it have been her father? She was sure she was hallucinating, so weary with the travel and the pace of this mission that she was starting to imagine faces and voices from her past. The voice could have been his, and the medal was the same as the one he'd been so proud of when she was a girl. But why him? He was not someone she'd expect to see at this moment. He'd made a career in diplomacy and had been involved in his share of espionage, but it was all part of official business. And he'd retired from the Russian diplomatic corps years ago.

She stared at the men on the screen, now unsure about two of them. Her daughter's father and now her own father—if indeed it was them—and both working with Shi. What incentives had Shi offered? What buttons had he pushed? They had no great love for America, but they had never spoken of themselves as its enemy. Yet here they seemed to be, plotting something. No doubt they were complicit in the traffic control attack on the west coast, and no doubt they all now knew that the advantage they'd gained through the use of the stowaway chips would soon be over. Word had been put out to every known client of Network Systems about the infiltration, and the affected servers were being taken offline. But what if other companies' equipment had been similarly compromised before it was delivered? Stokes was probably right again—they were going to make one more move.

Yvonne worked on linking to the GPS satellite. It would be reading the same signal as she was. In a minute she had the coordinates of the Afghan end of the exchange.

She listened carefully to their conversation as they discussed final preparations and the expected effect of their action. Whatever they were planning would be executed at two-thirty local time, just a few minutes from then. Mahmud's team would initiate two attacks simultaneously, to double the chance of success and show the depth of their reach into America's electronic infrastructure. Then the U.S. government would be contacted and presented with a price to prevent further attacks. One billion dollars. They would have until morning to wire the funds into the first of the secret accounts, where it would be instantly laundered through a dozen paths, until no longer traceable. The money could be used for terrorist weapons, or could fund further cyber espionage. Some of it, she was sure, would line Shi's pockets.

Their voices sounded almost angry to her, as though they had been forced to take this action. She sensed it would be something more than another simple probe—this one would do some permanent damage somewhere. Shi suggested they would have something to toast when it was over. Then the man in Puli Khumri laughed and said, "I guess I will have to break my sacred vows."

It was what Farris used to say when she knew him. Back then it was a joke he reprised whenever he was preparing for a wild time— a joke to make fun of the religion he'd been raised in. Now, from what she saw, he'd embraced that religion again, but in a violently fundamentalist way. In that philosophy it was wrong to drink alcohol, but not to celebrate a jihadist act, no matter how many people it hurt.

Yvonne's body pulsed with fear as she watched her former lover coordinate mayhem, maybe murder, with the coolness of a Wall Street financier. He had always been so gentle when they were together, always a proponent for peace, arguing against the hardliners in his family who preached violence. He had been so supportive when she became pregnant with Lillian that she seriously considered letting him take care of her when she got involved with serious hacking, instead of sending her back to the Russian side of her family. She realized it would have made no difference—if that really was her father on the other end of the line, and he was part of this scheme, poor Lilly would have been exposed to this evil no matter who she stayed with.

Now Yvonne began to think of her daughter, how she'd essentially abandoned her in her adolescence to join the ranks of cyber warriors. Some mother she'd been. She couldn't maintain a relationship, went through men like they were toys. Her daughter was practically grown up, and yet if they'd met on the street, Lilly might not even recognize her.

She had to focus. She reminded herself how late it was, how little sleep she'd had in the past few days. These were not thoughts to be having during a crisis. She contacted Stokes on his cell, using the radio feature. She needed his help, his guidance. Unlike her, he hadn't been able to sleep, owing to the difficulty in adjusting to the time changes the team had been put through. "Don't worry. Still seems like afternoon to me," he said when she apologized for the call. He ran down the hall to her room when she told him what she'd latched on to.

"What are the targets?" he asked. "Is there still time to warn the U.S.?"

"I don't know," she said. "Whatever they've chosen was picked a while ago."

Mahmud asked if Shi had people in position to video the event for propaganda later. He brought up a pair of schematics, each with several points marked.

"What are those? Power grids?" Stokes said. He moved in over Yvonne's shoulder to take a closer look. On each tiny image, a series of lines radiated from a central locus, intersecting almost haphazardly, some circling back on themselves, others heading straight towards the ends of the drawing.

"Can't be power grids," Yvonne said. "There's a different logic to it."

"Wait a minute," Stokes said. "You said whatever they're planning is going to happen at two-thirty Kabul time." He looked at his watch. "I haven't changed the time since we left San Francisco. Add three hours to this, minus the half hour difference here, and that makes it around six on the east coast… Right in the middle of holiday traffic."

"It's the highway system? How can they affect that?"

"Not highways. Railroad tracks."

Yvonne figured it out too. "If they have access to Amtrak's computer system, they can command the switching functions. They can switch the tracks so two trains head straight into each other. Hundreds of people could die."

"The government will be forced to pay the ransom."

"Which cities, Rohan? Do you recognize the maps?"

"I only know it's not D.C. But it could be Boston, Philly... There's too many cities on the east coast to know."

"And we don't have time to download and go through every map."

"How much time do we have?"

"Maybe fifteen or twenty minutes."

He pulled out his cell, but put it back. "I can't be sure I can get through to CyberCom in time. Even if I did, they don't have time to warn anyone. I'd better get Magadan out of bed." He opened the door to leave, but paused for a second and smiled. "Funny," he said. "A few hours ago I would have figured that would be your job."

"Rohan, stop."

"It was just a joke..."

"No. I mean, don't get the general. He may not want to help us right now. Not after what I did to him."

"What you did to him?"

"Maybe I should say what I didn't do to him. And by the time we explain what's going on, it will be too late. Get Colin instead. I have a better idea."

The transmission among Mahmud and his partners ended. Stokes looked as though he was about to say something, but stopped and went down the hallway to retrieve Colin. The noise had awakened the rest of the team, and Stokes filled them in on the way back.

"Colin, come sit by me," she said.

"Well, I thought you'd never ask."

"Why do men always have to get sexual in a crisis?" She kept typing, not bothering to look at him. "Can you still fly a drone?"

"Kidding? I could do it in my sleep. And I've got just the thing to make this work." He bolted out the door and down the hall. In a few seconds he was back, carrying a joystick.

"You take that when you travel?" Woody asked.

"Hey, you just never know when you'll need one… Plug me in, baby!"

"What are you doing, Yvonne?" Stokes asked.

"Do you remember when you told the general about my role in writing the Reaper software?"

"Sure."

"Well, I never told you that I left a little extra code in the string."

"What do you mean?"

"A back door," she said. "A way to slip in unnoticed and take command of the system." She typed a few more lines and sat back. "There. I'm in."

A picture resolved of the tarmac outside.

Colin took control of the Reaper. A few keystrokes to start the engine, and he guided it quickly to an open runway. It was in the air before anyone on the ground could stop it. A siren sounded outside. They could hear jet engines coming to life.

"Fly to the coordinates, Col," Yvonne said. "When you get close, we'll make a decision whether to go in. Maybe we'll get lucky and see a satellite dish on the roof."

"How much time, kids?" Buck asked.

"Fifteen minutes. Maybe," Yvonne said.

"Cutting it damn close. You won't have time to do any sightseeing."

Colin kept the drone low, using radar to stay close to the terrain and away from any pursuing jets. Infrared imaging gave him a decent picture of the ground below. Everyone in the room watched as the drone covered miles of empty, black landscape.

Stokes broke the silence. "Tell me more about this back door, Yvonne. Tell me why."

"Let's just say I was still having doubts about my role with you and CyberCom. I wanted something I could exploit later if I changed my mind."

"Even after I spoke up for you at CIA? I kept you out of prison. I gave you a future."

"And I am eternally grateful for that, darling," she said. "But things change, Rohan. Situations. Relationships. I couldn't take that chance."

"And now?"

He was angry. She could see that she'd damaged the trust he placed in her. "And now things have changed again," she said.

"What does that mean?"

She checked the status of the drone as Colin worked the joystick. She would not answer Stokes. "I'm amazed no one ever found my signature in the code," she said instead.

Colin jerked the stick hard. "They're on us already. I've got two jets on my tail," he said.

"They'll try to shoot it down," Stokes said. "They don't know what it's doing. For all they know it's been hijacked by terrorists."

"Colin, can you avoid them?"

"You bet. This thing is designed to elude radar. And all those hours of online flight will come in handy."

They watched as he maneuvered the drone left and right, as close to the rocky terrain as he could go. "Kind of tough on such a small screen, but we're a pretty small target. And it's damn dark out there. At least we have that on our side."

Cannon fire appeared on the laptop monitor as streaks of light, passing close to the drone's port side and raised billows of dust on the ground below. One of the jets released a Sidewinder that closed on the drone in seconds. The missile missed to the right and slammed into the side of a mountain. "They'll have to be pretty lucky to hit us," Colin said.

"We'll have to be pretty lucky to get away with this," Nigel corrected.

"If we can get close to the buildings, they'll have to pull off," Colin said. "Without knowing our target they can't take a chance on firing and killing people on the ground."

"Yeah, let's just hope there are some buildings out there. This place is a wasteland," Woody said.

But there were a few structures. It was barely a town, but enough buildings for Colin to shelter the Reaper. The U.S. jets broke off their attack.

"I'm almost on top of the coordinates you gave me," Colin said. "Time to arm the missiles."

"You sure you want to do this, Yvonne? I know how anti-violence you are," Buck said.

"They're trying to kill hundreds of people, Buck. That's the kind of violence I'm against." His point bothered her, though. In her years of hacking and espionage since that first incident at the hotel, she had never physically hurt anyone, let alone kill. Every job was about money, and it was always taking from people or a government that could afford the loss. Now she was responsible for sending missiles on their way to kill a man—the father of her child, and whoever was with him, whether complicit or uninvolved. There was no choice. She imagined facing her daughter when the news of what she'd done reached Lilly.

"Time?" Buck asked.

Yvonne looked at the monitor. "Like, now," she said.

Colin yelled, "No!"

"What's wrong?"

"The missiles won't arm."

Yvonne leaned in and tried to help.

"We stole an empty bird," Colin said.

Stokes moved in close and put his hand on Colin's shoulder. "Take the drone in," he said.

"Are you serious? That's a ten million dollar bird."

"We have no choice. I'll take the responsibility. Go in on my authorization."

Yvonne turned to him. "Rohan, is it enough?"

"A thirty-six-foot craft and a load of fuel… it had better be."

Colin glanced at her. "You're sure about these coordinates?"

Was she? What if the numbers were off? Without the missiles even a degree could mean the difference between destroying the target or killing innocent people on the ground—or losing the lives of hundreds of Americans back home. There was no time to recheck. The technology was proven. The numbers never lied, never played favorites. She had used them her entire career and they had never let her down, and she trusted them more than she trusted any person. If there had been any failures, they had been due to human error, someone making a judgment when one wasn't necessary, basing a decision on a feeling, instead of the data, the numbers. Her computer told her this was where the attack was emanating. "Yes, I am," she said.

The screen showed a bland rectangle of a house in the infrared light. There was nothing special about it, nothing to set it apart from the few neighbor homes in the vicinity. There were no guards with rifles posted on the roof, no dish they could see, and no indication that this was anything more than a simple dwelling.

"Pray we've made the right call."

Colin slid the stick forward. The monitor showed the house rushing towards it. Windows became visible. Lights were on in one of the rooms.

And the screen went black.

"Whoever lived there doesn't live there anymore," Woody said.

There was no applause or cheers. Everyone in the room continued to stare at the screen, even though there was nothing to see. The only way they could confirm the hit was to call CyberCom and ask if terrorists had struck in the states. Stokes pulled out his cell again, but couldn't get a signal. "They've probably shut down unauthorized communications," he said.

Yvonne tried to reach CyberCom through her laptop. "At least the general's access is still authorized," she said.

They heard what sounded like trucks pulling up by the guest quarters. The front door banged open. Shouts echoed through the hallway as a security team ran towards the room. Woody and Silk took up positions on either side of the door, but Buck told them not to make the situation worse. Still, Woody hovered at the doorway, if only to intimidate.

Six men, armed with rifles, ordered everyone out. When Yvonne kept working the laptop, one of them lowered his M-16 at her. Stokes pulled her chair away from the table and made sure she complied, dragging her by the arm into the hall, where Magadan was waiting for both of them.

The general was less than pleased at being awakened in the middle of the night. "It's all very clear now," he said. "Show the general a little skin and pick off his passwords."

Stokes said, "Mags, this is no time to go by the book. People in the U.S. would have died. We had to hack the drone. There wasn't time to do it any other way."

"Why? What was going to happen?"

Stokes told him about the communication they'd picked up and the threat to the Amtrak system.

"My boys had that too. We were analyzing."

"And you would have figured it out in a few hours," Yvonne said. "By then a thousand Americans would have been dead."

Magadan stared at her with a look that said he didn't believe she cared about Americans.

"By the time we could have convinced you of the threat, it would have been too late to react," Stokes said. "I take full responsibility for the action."

"I have a hard time believing this was all your idea," Magadan said.

"I gave the orders. Yvonne and Colin followed them. Everyone else was just watching. You want to take anyone into custody—here I am." He put his wrists out.

The general signaled to his men to move in. "You're all under arrest right now. We'll figure out who's responsible later. I hope you realize how serious this offense is."

Buck and Nigel allowed themselves to be cuffed, but Silk grabbed the arms of the guard who was attempting to chain him. Another airman seized him from behind. Woody moved towards both guards, but stopped when the muzzle of a rifle pointed at his temple.

Yvonne started to speak, but a man's voice from the laptop cut her off. "Rohan, is that you?"

"Sir. Yes, it's me."

"Who's with you? Is that the lovely Yvonne Tran? And General Magadan, too. You kids are out awfully late for a school night."

The general moved close to the screen. "Admiral Lucas, your agents were apprehended after hijacking a U.S. Air Force drone and using it to attack a location in a residential area about fifty miles from here. Did you have any knowledge of this action?"

"Mags, I understand what you're doing, but I want you to let them go. On my authorization," Lucas said.

"Sir, I'll need that in writing through a secure channel."

"Already on its way," Lucas said.

Stokes said, "Sir, is everyone back there all right?"

"We tapped into the same communication as you a few minutes before the attack was supposed to have been launched. They were targeting Philly and Chicago. There was no way we could have stopped it from here.

Colin leaned over to see the monitor. "Ah, sir? Did we get 'em?"

"Satellite images show the building was destroyed. Whatever was inside went with it. But they also show a vehicle leaving the scene. Could have been Mahmud, but we don't know."

Magadan still wasn't satisfied. "Sir, whether you condone these actions or not, the fact is these people stole and destroyed a ten million dollar piece of technology…"

"Easy, general," the admiral said. "Did I happen to mention the communication you will be receiving is co-signed by the secretary of defense?"

The general signaled his men to free Buck and the others. When he was loose, Woody took the handcuffs from the airman guarding him, and twisted one of the ends backwards into an S shape before handing it back.

The director went on. "Let these folks get a good night's rest. In the morning, give them clearance to take off and an escort until they reach the Indian Ocean. I assume, Mr. Ryan, that you'll be delivering your aircraft to your client a little late?"

Buck said, "If you wouldn't mind, sir, don't mention this little side trip to them."

"I'll keep it a secret."

"Hey," Colin said. "Looks like we'll be able to make the New Year's party back at Finnegan's after all."

"Right," Stokes said. "Yvonne, you going to play that ukulele?"

She rolled her eyes. "Balalaika, Rohan. How many times do I have to tell you?"

"Hang on, Rohan." It was Lucas again. "I hate to have you miss the party, but you've got a few questions to answer. I'll expect you in my office as soon as you're stateside."

Chapter Thirteen - Epilogue

11:50 p.m., December 31, Finnegan's Wake, Key West

Yvonne had never tried to play Auld Lang Syne on the balalaika before, but in the noise and drunken revels of the New Year's Eve party at Finnegan's, no one could tell how far her rendition was from the original. She strummed, but the only person who seemed interested was Colin, who rested his chin in his hands while he gazed at Yvonne.

The rest of the crowd was less concerned with music, and more concerned with whom they might welcome in the New Year. Buck had brought the team to the party after delivery of the Boeing (with an explanation about the damage to the tail) to his clients. Silk was proving as deft at scoring in this world as in that of aircraft snatching, and had gone off to a corner with a woman Yvonne's age—which had her wondering if there had been some attraction all along.

Woody hardly needed to try. The big man was surrounded by Key West party babes, and was having his fun lifting two at a time—one hanging from each hand—in military press style. The count was twenty reps and still going.

Buck was at a table, drinking with her friend Dutch Sock. Nigel was the real surprise. Last time Yvonne looked, he was in a clinch with Rachel. It looked like both would need a New Year's resolution to live down that escapade.

A few minutes before midnight they all came together at Yvonne's table. Buck, Silk and Woody all gave her a hug, which surprised Sock, but there would be no explanations for those who hadn't been on the mission. They would leave the others guessing as to the events and emotions involved. The memories would have to be private, since the CyberCom director had sworn them to silence regarding the activities of the past week. It was better that way, too—the mission would be catalogued in that part of memory that held special, unspoken meaning, the kind that could be brought back years from now and still retain an impact.

Buck spoke over the din of the crowd. "You know," he said, "I'm almost sorry that our little trip is over. It was a blast working with you. Most exciting trip I've been on in years."

Silk raised his glass. "Ready to do it again, whenever you are, Yvonne."

She picked up her drink and held it to toast. "Here's to the one member of our group who couldn't make it." Stokes had flown straight to Washington once they got back to the states. His abandonment of his office to join the others, and his actions afterwards had put his position at CyberCom in serious jeopardy. Yvonne hadn't heard a word from him for days. Perhaps he'd been fired and was too embarrassed to tell anyone. She would have to try to call him tomorrow.

With a minute to go until midnight, the crowd began to pair off for the New Year's toast. Colin sidled up to her, and moved his chair until their knees were touching. "A New Year," he said. "Lots of new possibilities."

She hoped it was true, but maybe not in the same way as he thought. CyberCom had yet to determine if Farris Mahmud was still alive. His status might be a factor in her future work. And what of the third man on the conversation she'd hacked into in Afghanistan? She hadn't been able to shake the idea that it was her father, connected somehow to an alliance dedicated to terrorizing the United States.

She thought of him, the regal figure she knew as a child, having changed so completely from a dedicated government official into a ruthless criminal, ready to sacrifice hundreds of lives to extort money from her adopted country. It simply couldn't be.

She thought of her daughter, Lillian. It had been years since she'd seen her.

And she thought of Stokes again.

Partiers watched the second hand on the big wall clock as it passed thirty seconds to go. Yvonne could feel the vibration of the crowd. But no, it was her cochlear implant, pulsing against her jaw. Then her smart phone rang. It had to be Stokes, of course.

"This is your conscience, Yvonne," he began. "I advise you to be careful how you welcome in the New Year."

"Rohan, darling. You're missing the most wonderful party. Everyone is here."

"Unavoidable, Yvonne," he said. "The director had some tough questions for me. I've been debriefing for days."

"I can barely hear you over the noise," she said. Fifteen seconds to go. The crowd began to count down the numbers. She heard them reverberate through the bar. Ten, nine, eight...

Stokes shouted, "I met with the president."

"Yes," she said. "I wish you were present here too."

"No! The president! He has something in mind for us. For the team. Another mission."

"Mission?" she said. "What about the mission?"

The crowd cheered, drowning Stokes out.

"Rohan! What are you talking about? Did you say you talked to the president?"

She couldn't hear him—the connection had been broken—and she looked up from the phone. Colin was staring at her with his usual bedroom eyes. The crowd was still celebrating. She looked up at the clock to see that midnight had come and gone. It was a New Year, but it didn't quite feel like one. In fact, she had the feeling that the residue of the last one was still affecting her life.

Everyone was still drinking, content to let the festivities go on forever. But Yvonne left her glass on the table as she dialed Stokes's number back.

Authors

Mike Brennan is founder of Michigan News Network, and serves as Editor & Publisher of MITechNews.Com. Brennan has worked since 1980 as a technology business writer at newspapers in New York City, San Jose, CA., Seattle, WA., Memphis, TN., and Detroit, MI. He co-founded and served as managing editor of Seattle-based Pacific Rim News Service, which developed a network of more than 100 freelance journalists in 17 Asia-Pacific countries.

Brennan earned a bachelor's degree from the University of Michigan, a master's degree in journalism from the University of Missouri and was the 1992-93 Knight Fellow in Economic Journalism at the University of Michigan.

Brennan has covered cyber security news for the past decade. For the last five years he has partnered with cyber security expert Richard Stiennon, publisher of IT-Harvest. Brennan lives on a lake in West Michigan, where he was born and raised.

Gian DeTorre is the pen name of an award winning fiction writer and literary critic whose work has been published in the U.S. and internationally.

The cyber security technology featured in the novella has been verified by security expert Richard Stiennon, Chief Research Analyst at IT-Harvest. Stiennon has been in the security field since 1995. He is the author of *Surviving Cyberwar* and technology consultant to *Cyber Styletto*, the first of a series of novellas that will chronicle today's very dangerous Internet world.